For the Love of Christmas

Four Stories with a Southern Flair

Mary Marvella

M. Barfield Publishing

Cover Design:	Melba Moon
Photography:	Deposit Photos
Interior:	My thanks to MJ Flournoy
Editor:	M. Barfield

Table of Contents

A Very Bella Thanksgiving

Mary Marvella

This trip from Birmingham seemed both longer and short than the last time Anna had driven this route. This time she was headed home for Thanksgiving. Five years ago she had been eighteen and pregnant. So much had changed. Bella's angelic voice sang "Jesus Loves Me" from the back seat. Nothing pleased the mama in Anna more than hearing her child sing, but her daughter had sung since they left her apartment an hour ago and showed no signs of dozing off. At least it kept both of them awake.

"Baby, could you sing something else for a while?"

"Yes, ma'am! "

Seeing her nod in the rearview mirror, Anna braced herself. Bella's grin warned Anna that she should have been more specific.

That angelic voice shouted, "Something else, something else" to the tune of "Jesus Loves Me."

She tried to outlast Bella, but after ten minutes she gave up. "As lovely as this song is, could you sing a different song from Sunday School?"

"Yes, Mama. Granny loves 'Jesus Loves the Little Children'. "

"That would be nice."

Outside of Montgomery the singer stopped singing to whine, "I'm sooo hongry, I could eat the south end of a north bound mu-el."

Anna struggled not to laugh at the expression Bella had learned from her grandpa. "Eat the gold fish in your baggie."

"Ma-ma! Then I'll be sooo thirrr-sty!"

"Drink the juice in your Sippy cup."

"Then I'll haff to go to the baffroom!" The hands in the air shrug was so Bella and so true.

Since Anna had been sipping iced tea from her own adult Sippy cup a break sounded like a good idea. She wasn't giving in to her daughter, she really needed to stop.

As though Bella had read her mind she bounced and shouted "McDonald's, one mile!" She could read well, so Anna thanked her lucky stars Bella wasn't reading all the signs beside the road. Otherwise, she'd have to answer questions about grown up stuff to a kid who wasn't in school yet.

As Anna pulled off the highway and into a McDonald's parking lot her cell rang. She punched the speaker on her steering wheel to avoid hearing Bella whine to talk to Granny. "Hi, Mama."

"Hey, Granny! We're coming to have Thanksgivin' with you and Grandpa!" Bella freed herself from her seatbelt faster than Houdini could have and scrambled over the seat like a monkey. "I'm so happy! I missed you!

"I missed you, too, Bella Bambina," Mama said, laughing as she always did when she said the name of Bella's favorite cartoon character. Mama refused to call her Caroline, which suited Bella just fine. When her grandpa told her that Bella meant beautiful, she insisted everyone call her Bella, even her preschool teachers. Who was the kid's mama to argue with the such logic?

Anna managed to let her mama know they would need stops and would not arrive in Stoneridge in the five to six hours it took her daddy to make the drive, even allowing for bathroom breaks and leg stretching.

Bella danced her way into McDonald's, her strawberry blonde curls bouncing, and entertained the four people in line and anyone else who could see her. "I'm goin to see my granny and grandpa!" She twirled. 'I'm goin' to ---"

Anna clamped her hand over the tiny mouth that

7

could alert any weirdo that she and the child were travelling and where. Indignant, Bella opened her mouth as if to bite the offending hand, probably a reflex action, but Anna leaned low and whispered in her ear, "Don't you dare!"

Twenty minutes later they had stopped in two of the restroom stalls and washed their hands enough to kill every germ in Alabama and Georgia. Bella had eaten her kid's meal and half of Anna's fries. She'd be wound up, but maybe riding would lull her to sleep for a while. *Dream on.*

The next leg in the trip lasted another hour with Bella reading every book they'd put in her Princess backpack. After the potty stop Bella glued herself to the iPad indulgent grandparents had given her for Christmas and watched cartoons and recorded shows about monkeys eating and sharing bananas and dancing eggs and trees counting and adding. Anna tried not to allow herself to wonder about how the aunts and uncles would react to Bella and which would ask about her daddy. No one, not even her parents, knew who had fathered her beautiful child, and she'd keep it that way as long as she could. Even now John-Paul's green eyes stared back from Bella's face when she had a question or wanted to argue about something. Her little chin tilted as his square jaw had when he wanted to make her know he disagreed with what she had said. Though she hadn't seen him since she left town, she remembered everything about him, too much about him.

His expression when she told him she changed her mind about going to Mercer with him came to her in her dreams many nights and on Bella's little face when she watched *Bambi* and *Ice Princess*.

She could no longer avoid going home since her daddy had enough chest pains to require a heart cath. She could leave town as soon as he was okay and back home with her mama and aunts on both sides there to help look after him. In three weeks max she could be in her own apartment, even if he needed a heart by-pass, and Bella could start practicing for the Nativity scene for the Christmas pageants at church.

Bella finally dozed off at the Georgia state line, but Anna's worries grew. What if Daddy was worse off than Mama had told her? She'd made the mistake of researching heart catheterizations and heart by-pass surgery, which had shown some cases that went wrong. Shaking her head, she pushed those bad situations to the back of her mind. Then, of course, she imagined running into her baby's father or his parents. Would his mama take one look at Bella and realize the little girl looked like her son had as a child? Would she and Bella have stayed away from home for nothing? At this point they couldn't bully her and their son into marriage. She had the strength to refuse now that she was no longer a pregnant teen and she had a life away from Stoneridge. He'd probably found someone who shared his goals and started

9

his own family by now. He might even have his own pulpit. She had made the right decision by not telling him about her pregnancy.

***

Anna had barely pulled into her parent's driveway when Bella woke and shouted. "We're here! We're here!"

Before Anna could say anything Daddy rose from his favorite rocking chair on the front porch and bounded down the steps. *Should he be doing that in his condition?*

Mama rushed through the front screen door. Wiping her hands on an apron Anna had made for her as part of a 4 H project, she hurried after Daddy. "Jason Bledsoe, what do you think you're doing? "

He didn't respond.

Bella unbuckled her seatbelt while Daddy opened the driver's door to hurry Anna out. Bella crawled over the front seat and over her mama. "Grandpa! I missed you!" she bubbled over, kissing her grandpa's cheeks, first one and then the other. "Get me out, please?" She stretched out the please.

Daddy did what he always did. He pulled her over Anna and leaned over to kiss Anna's cheek. "I'm so glad you came, Sugar Pie."

"You know better that to lift that child!" Mama scolded

him and reached for Bella, who leaned over to her granny.

"Granny!"

Mama took Bella and swung her around. "Let's get everyone inside for some iced tea and cookies."

Bella motioned for her Granny to lean down and then stage whispered, "I need to use the baffroom. "

"Of course you do," Mama said.

Daddy rushed up the stairs and ahead of everyone so he could hold the door open. When Mama Anna glared at him he shrugged. "I was raised to be a gentleman. Get over it. I'm not an invalid."

Walking into her childhood home made her want to laugh and cry for years she'd missed being here. The vanilla fragrance of sugar cookies made her stomach grumble. She knew from memory they'd be soft and gooey, the way she loved them. Everything looked and felt the same, but photos of her with Bella and the two of them with her parents decorated the hall and the mantle. Good thing Mama had a framing shop at one time and knew how to arrange frames on walls and everywhere without making space seem cluttered. Both parents had bragging albums made for themselves and for her and Bella. The number of wall portraits made her shake her head. Staying away from home hadn't kept folks from seeing her child's face. Folks must have speculated over each feature. The story was that she'd met a guy as soon as she got to college for summer school. They might think she was *easy,* but they wouldn't know the son of their *Hell-fire-and-damnation* preacher was the father of an *out-of-wedlock* child. And he hadn't had to marry her and skip college or be disowned for causing a scandal. Even in this time when many young folks had sex young and women raised babies alone, her church was still old fashioned. There would have been a wedding, or Hell to pay, or both. Her parents had been disappointed that she wouldn't tell the truth, but they adored Bella. His parents might not have been so loving and accepting. Shaking her head to push memories aside, she turned to the present.

"Daddy, why didn't you tell me you were sick? Shouldn't you have the cath procedure right away?" Her stomach flipped at the thought of what he would go through. She hugged him and clung for dear life. He was her rock. With her cheek against his chest she could hear his heart beating, loud and strong.

"No, Sugar Pie." He squeezed her and leaned back. He winked at her. "My doctor is out of town for Thanksgiving. He said Monday would be soon enough, as long as I don't play football, or wrestle, or pick up heavy stuff. And no, my grandchild isn't heavy, but I won't carry her for a while after the procedure."

A bundle of energy skipped into the den. "Mama!

Granny got the best baffroom!" Bella's arms spread wide and the close. "It's got special little soap, like flowers," She used her fingers to show shape and size. "and a funny sink and everything is white and shiny! Can we make ours white, too?"

"We'll see about it."

Grabbing Anna's hand, Bella pulled her toward the kitchen. "Granny said she had cookies in here and they smell so good!"

Her daddy scooted ahead to open swinging door to the kitchen. "Thanks, Daddy."

The kitchen was still yellow and green and white, but shiny, as though someone had painted recently. Bella checked all the chairs and giggled when she found one with a small ladder and a red box with stars around the sides on the seat. She clapped and danced around the chair and then climbed onto the box.

"What makes you think that's your seat?" Mama asked, keeping her expression close to serious.

Bella shook her head and crossed her arms. "My name is on the box, silly goose."

"That's our Bella!" Daddy said and kissed her cheek before he pulled Mama's chair out on one side of his and then Anna's on his other side. Those had always been their places at the table. She'd even carved her name in inch high letters on the edge. It hadn't been easy with a nail file. That trick has cost her a month of television and a lot of mopping the floor.

Mama had put a plate of cookies and glasses of iced tea on the round wooden table. Anna reached for the small glass beside Bella's place with the intention of swapping it for her sippy cup. She pulled her hand back when she noticed the lid and straw.

A knock stopped Bella from biting the cookie headed for her mouth. "We got company." Anna grabbed Belle mid scramble to head to the door as official greeter.

Aunt Josephine breezed in before Daddy could rise. Her short brown curls had more silver than Anna remembered her having. "Don't get up! I couldn't wait to see our Anna and her little Bella." She swooped down to smother Anna in a hug that enveloped her in White Shoulders and big bosom.

Bella piped up, "Who's the big lady hugging my mama?"

Aunt Josephine released Anna and turned toward Bella's chair. "Oh, my goodness gracious!" She rounded the table and put her hands on the cherub's chubby cheeks. "Aren't you just the cutest thing! You look like your mama did at your age!"

"Really? Mama said I look like a princess. Did she look like a princess?"

"She did, indeed. We called her Princess Anna." Josephine used her dear-sweet-aunt voice that charmed kids. It had charmed Anna for as long as she could remember.

"Call me Aunt Jo-Jo, you precious girl!

Anna could almost hear the wheels turning as her aunt catalogued Bella's doll-like features, green eyes, and expansive mannerisms. By tomorrow every woman in town would have heard about little Bella and have a clear enough image of her to sketch her face. Aunt Josephine wasn't cruel. She was just nosy and considered it her duty to spread information. Since the story was that Bella's daddy wasn't from here, maybe the ladies wouldn't study the high school yearbooks to find a man Bella resembled. She should be so lucky.

Aunt Jo-Jo made friends with Bella by pulling suckers and hard candy from her apron pocket, another of Anna's 4 H projects. She had made two more aprons. Would Aunt Marla be wearing hers tomorrow for Thanksgiving dinner? Surely Aunt Melly wouldn't have packed hers to go to visit her college friend before coming here.

"I just can't decide." Bella struck her hands on her cheeks pose. *Little show-off.* Then she went in for the kill.

She put her tiny hands on Aunt Jo-Jo's face and rolled her green eyes. "If I can have all the candy, I promise to eat only one piece now and save the rest. Please?"

"Bella, don't be greedy. Choose one thing. Aunt Jo-Jo night want to save the other candy for another child."

Bella gave her a *get real* look. "Mama, she brought the candy when she came to see me."

Daddy snorted, Mama hid her grin, and Jo-Jo burst out laughing.

Anna kept a straight face. "She probably came to see me, her niece, or Granny, her sister, or Grandpa, who will have a procedure Monday."

Bella scrunched her little face for a minute, apparently mulling over the idea that she might not be the main attraction here. "She sat by me and offered me candy. I think she came to see me."

She probably got that one right.

Aunt Jo-Jo's booming belly laugh ruined any chance of anyone but Bella winning that round. She handed the candy and gum to the satisfied little princess.

Anna held her hand out to Bella, who put all but the gum in her mother's hand. "I'm saving the candy. Granny said the cookies on the table were for us and I want one. "

Granny laughed. "Yep. I said we could each have one

before supper if Bella promised to eat her supper. "

Bella nodded and wiggled on her throne. "I promised!" She turned to Anna. "Mama, you gotta eat your supper, too."

"I promise. No dieting at my mama's house."

Aunt Jo-Jo stood. "Gotta go finish my desserts for tomorrow."

Anna stood, too, and hugged her aunt.

"I am so glad you can be with us this year, sweetie!" her aunt said. "We've missed you."

"I missed you, too, Aunt Jo-Jo." And she had missed her family, but for good reason.

"Will you go with us for the Christmas parade and the Christmas tree lighting Saturday?"

Bella bounced and clapped. "Say yes, Mama!"

"I'm not sure." She really didn't need to take Bella to the town square where everyone in town would be.

"We'll see. Grandpa might want to stay home and rest."

Her daddy gave her a raised eyebrow look but said nothing.

Mama's homemade chicken tenders pleased everyone, even though Daddy's weren't fried. Bella even ate the oven baked breaded veggie sticks. Mama had gone

17

through a lot of trouble to please the little girl and her husband, whose meals contained lots of healthy versions of good food.

When Bella started to squirm Daddy stood and took his plate to the sink. He reached for Anna's, but she grabbed it.

"Aren't you supposed to rest? I'll help Mama with the dishes."

He shook his head and walked around the table to Bella. "Do you need to go to the bathroom, Princess"

She nodded. He grabbed her under the arms and set her on the floor. She dashed through the kitchen door and he followed. "I'll read to her while you and your mama talk and wash dishes."

"Thanks, Daddy." Anna kissed his cheek.

"Bella and I are pals. She likes to read to me. Bossy little dickens, just like her mama."

Washing dishes took little time, since Mama always washed up as she cooked. For the past five years her parents had to come to her the day after Thanksgiving and Christmas, to celebrate a day late so the main family had holiday meals together and she and Bella had family holidays. So far Bella hadn't commented on the change of days. She was fine as long as Santa came the right day.

She'd had two Christmases each and plenty of toys. She probably thought that was the way everyone did things.

***

By the time Anna carried sleepy Bella to bed she paused for a second at her old bedroom door. The room looked the way she'd left it, with same matching lavender bed spread and curtains. The purple and white throw pillows perched against lavender pillow shams. A small bed fit for a little princess sat near the head of her old bed. When she tried to put Bella into the small bed the child protested and clung to Anna like a little monkey. Tired and in need of a shower, she put her daughter in the big bed. Thank goodness her mama had bathed Bella earlier. She'd move the child after her own shower. Framed photos of her with John-Paul sat on her dresser. Why hadn't she removed them when she left for college? She grabbed her night shirt and pajama bottom and toothbrush from the small suitcase she'd packed. She made it to the door, but she turned around and put the photos of her with Bella's daddy into a dresser drawer. Maybe the kiddo hadn't noticed them and would have no questions about the man in the pictures with her mama.

The fruity scents of her old shampoo and baby shampoo made Anna laugh as she walked into her old bathroom. Someone had painted and spruced up this room, but it had clearly been waiting for her return. Seeing her favorite shampoo and conditioner made her smile. Mama had bought new bottles and tubes of all the products she'd used five years ago. Bella's favorite shampoo, bath bubbles, tooth paste, and a new toothbrush sat proudly by hers. She felt a little guilty for staying away so long but not too guilty. She'd had a daughter to protect from nosey people. A hot shower left her muscles like Jello!

Back in her bedroom, she tried to move Bella to the child's bed, but she gave up when the little dickens wrapped arms and legs around her and clung. The fragrance of clean little girl won her over. This would be the first night Bella would sleep in a strange room in a strange bed. Tomorrow she'd tempt the kidlet into the bed bought just for her.

***

Anna stretched and yawned. No small arms or legs bound her body like an octopus. No little hands shook her head, trying to wake her. She kind of missed the usual nose-to-nose wake-up attempts that greeted her most mornings but not enough to get up yet. Frying bacon and baking turkey made her stomach growl and her mouth water. Mama had given her orders to sleep late, since the kitchen would be crowded my seven.

She and Mama and Aunt Melly had prepared holiday meals and had worked like a team, first in Melly's house and then in Anna's apartment. Mama and her aunts had always prepared big meals like a team and shooed her from the kitchen. Tempted to turn over and go back to sleep with her face on a pillow that smelled of Mama's fabric softener, she gave in to her curiosity about what her daughter was doing and her grumbling stomach.

Within minutes she'd brushed her teeth after checking to make sure Bella's toothbrush was damp and had toothpaste left on it. That kid would skip brushing if she could get by with it. Grabbing a brush and scrunchie from a drawer beside the bathroom sink, she swept her hair into a high ponytail. A touch of blush and lip gloss made her feel she'd get fewer comments about how she didn't look like she was taking care of herself or eating enough. Her aunts willingly commented on everything. Her jeans fit perfectly and showed little fading and her red shirt looked festive. On the way downstairs she heard childish giggling and voices she loved and had missed. Her aunts had arrived and started preparing for heavy eating. She swung into the kitchen and got hugs and a breakfast plate.

With each hug she got the *You're-too-skinny*" comment. Mama shooed her out. "Your daddy's waiting on the sun porch. He wanted to have breakfast with you. There's coffee and juice waiting. "

"Where's my Bella? I need a morning kiss."

Aunt Melly laughed loudly. "She's licking the beaters from my chocolate pie."

"Mama, I'm here." Bella giggled when Aunt Jo-Jo moved from in front of the little girl with chocolate on her face. "I need a morning kiss!"

Careful not to spill her food, Anna wove through the buxom bodies of her mama and her aunts and leaned into give Bella a careful kiss.

Bella kissed her cheek and grinned. "You got chocolate on your face!"

"So do you, Bella, and on your shirt!" Anna laughed, wishing for her cell phone to grab a picture.

"We all took pictures," Mama said, as though she'd read Anna's mind. "I already put mine on Facebook. Now go eat your breakfast before it gets cold."

Anna turned and headed toward the porch with her food. She hadn't even considered that Bella's photos would be on Facebook. She'd been careful about that for four years. Had her parents been posting photos for long? How long had they even been on Facebook? The enclosed porch had always been one of her favorite places. She could almost smell the fresh air and hear the birds outside.

Pausing, she watched her daddy spread pear preserves on wheat toast. "Morning, Daddy." She gave him a peck on his smooth-shaved cheek. He was still an Old Spice man as her pawpaw before him had been. Years ago she had given Daddy popular designer fragrances, but he'd stuck to his favorite brand.

"Good morning, Sugar Pie!" He poured her a cup of coffee from the Carafe on the glass topped table.

While she added enough milk to make it lighter than chocolate milk he put tomato slices on her plate. She took a bite of scrambled eggs, tomato, and grits. "How long has Mama been on Facebook?"

"A few months. Why? She and her sisters have found their old classmates and share photos and news there."

"That's nice." She'd get her phone from the bedroom and find how many friends they had. Maybe she worried about nothing.

Bella marched into the room and crawled into her lap. She snatched a piece of bacon and bit it. "I licked banana puddin', choclit pie, and some lemon cake bowls and beaters. I need somethin' salty."

"I'm sure you were a big help in the kitchen. Sugar Lump, could you go upstairs and get my phone and be really careful with it?" Anna asked.

Bella rolled her eyes and gave an exaggerated glare. "Of course I can. I'm not a baby." She flounced off and returned, holding the phone like a treasured glass vase. "Can we watch cartoons?"

Daddy took the plates and started for the kitchen.

"I can help." Bella grabbed a plate and followed him, walking slowly. One of these days she'd have to beg the kid for help. For now, Bella wanted to help with everything, which slowed a lot of chores.

Checking Facebook on her phone she found her mama's page. Lord have mercy, there were pictures of Anna as a kid, of Bella, and of her parents. Mama only had twenty-five friends. That could be a good thing. She started to type in John-Paul's name but stopped herself. She was better off not knowing about his life now.

Several times she stuck her head into the kitchen and offered to help, but the ladies shooed her away. At least she got to help prepare the meal when they celebrated at her place in Birmingham. Here she was as much a kid as Bella was. When she'd lived at home she hadn't cared. Now being left out felt odd.

Cousins drifted in at the last minute. Some brought dishes which they placed on the old breakfront as though they belonged here. The same Thanksgiving cloth Anna had loved covered the antique. Only two cousins came empty handed, Ben and Janice, Aunt Jo-Jo's daughter.

By the time everyone sat down to eat, the table

looked like a painting. Aunt Jo-Jo had made a centerpiece of fruit carved into flowers. Mama's dishes and stemware with hand painted flowers looked too festive to cover with food. Turkey and ham sat near Daddy's place so he could carve and slice, his specialties. If there had been one more dish on the table it would surely have collapsed.

Her cousins and their spouses had arrived in time to eat. Everyone made a big fuss over Bella, the only child in the bunch. Bella looked around the table and grinned. "I'm so hon-gry I could eat the South end of a noth-boun mu-el!"

Daddy opened his mouth but said nothing for seconds. Silence hung in the air, then everyone burst out laughing. "That's my little Bella."

Mama looked at her husband with that raised eyebrow look. "I told you little pictures have big ears."

When Daddy asked the blessing a lump in Anna's throat made swallowing difficult. She loved her family. *Please let us have a lot of years left together.*

Most of her aunts and cousins teased Anna as though they had not been apart for five years. No one asked questions, but she figured when the talk about Daddy's procedure was exhausted she'd be on the menu.

"So, how do you like Alabama?" Aunt Marla asked Anna.

"I've grown to love it." Anna looked at Bella, who looked ready to fall asleep on the throne Daddy had moved into the dining room earlier.

Aunt Melly smiled. "I've loved having this sweet girl near me. Bella has made me feel young again."

"I'm glad you could make time to come back for your daddy's heart procedure," Snotty Janice looked over her nose at Anna. "in case he---

"--- Of course I did." Anna tilted her tilted her head toward the little person who didn't need to hear talk about dying. "And Daddy will be just fine."

Janice pursed her lips. "I thought you were going to Mercer with John-Paul. Couldn't you get in?"

"Janice!" Aunt Jo-Jo frowned. "You know she got into Mercer. Something eatin' at you today?"

"No, just that little *Miss Perfect* stays away for five years and everybody acts like she's a Kardashian."

Anna glanced at Bella, who had perked up at Janice's nasal, whining voice. She rose quietly and walked over to Janice. She whispered, "Cousin, the child at this table doesn't need to watch an adult act like a nasty brat. Daddy doesn't need his meal spoiled. He has enough on his mind, as we all do. If you want to argue, wait until Bella's nap and I'll meet you out back. " Then she hugged Janice and sauntered back to her chair. Janice looked as though she had wallowed something nasty.

Bella looked at Janice. "My mama isn't a dasin. She's Anna."

Aunt Jo-Jo glared at her daughter. "Janice was kiddin' around, weren't you?"

Janice shrugged. "Yeah, kid, I was kiddin' around." Janice continued to eat, but Anna found little joy in the good food covering the table. Maybe she'd enjoy the leftovers later when Jealous Janice left.

Mama made sure Daddy ate the lower fat foods she'd prepared while Aunt Marla clucked over him like an older sister. Several folks ate the low fat dishes and enjoyed them enough to comment on how good they were and ask for recipes. Most of her family would be polite in any situation.

Talk around the table covered every topic but Anna's plans and the fatherless baby. Mama must have warned each person about mentioning the husband Anna had lost in an accident only months after their marriage and before Bella's birth. Who would believe that tale? Mama said it would work.

Daddy had warned her in a call before she headed home. "Sugar Pie, we love you and Bella more than anything, but your mama wanted to protect you and Bella from nosy folks, so she gave you a dead husband."

Janice ate like she was starved and then filled the containers she'd brought. Maybe she was extra nasty because she had money issues and couldn't afford to buy food, or maybe she was just frugal. Nah, she had always been greedy.

Bella followed her granddaddy into the den to watch a parade with the guys and Janice. The little munchkin be asleep in ten minutes in his lap. Anna helped clear the table and stacked dishes. She and her mama and Aunt Melly usually washed Melly's fine china and then her not so fine dishes, but here Mama and the aunts talked and worked together. Anyone would have thought the women were sisters by the way they worked in tandem.

Supper was a smaller event, since most cousins left to go to movies or even do some early shopping. It just didn't seem right to shop Thanksgiving night, even to grab bargains. She still counted pennies, but there were things she wouldn't do to save them.

***

Saturday Anna grabbed a scarf and sweatshirt for her and one for Bella. The day would warm up soon, but one could never tell, even in South Georgia. Mama had insisted they all watch the Christmas parade, so they piled into Anna's Mazda, since it was small and would be easier to park than her parent's behemoth of a Lincoln. Crowds had gathered on both sides of the courthouse square already, but folks moved aside to allow room for the children. Mama had wanted to bring a folding chair or stool for Daddy, but he'd dug in his heels. He said he felt fine.

The parade began with the Mayor Jake Stone waving from a convertible. Anna's excitement rose when she spotted the high school band, followed by the homecoming queen, who waved from a float on the bed of a flatbed truck. Bella's eyes lit up when she clapped and called out the name of a character from *Frozen*. The queen looked like her with her long blonde hair and white gown. The ladies in the court waved at the children. Anna had once been in the homecoming court. She hadn't thought about that in years.

"Mama, they waved at me!" Bella tried to twirl in the crowd but couldn't with her mama hanging onto her hand. No one complained. Small town folks were like that.

"Of course, they did," Anna called down to her.

The high school football team carried bags of candy. Anna recognized Ben, her youngest cousin, among the young men. He seemed to have grown since dinner two days ago. Bella waved at him and he waved back, tossing pieces of candy at her feet. She scrambled for the treasures.

She had never been so close to a parade, even a small one, and she was loving the excitement. She clapped when she spotted a huge float decorated with fake snow and

Christmas trees. Elves surrounded Santa in a sleigh pulled by fake reindeer. He waved and tossed candy. When the float passed Anna and her family, Santa seemed to pause for seconds, staring directly at her. Who was playing Santa now? It certainly wasn't the Santa she remembered. After seconds Santa resumed his waving and candy tossing and ho-ho-ing. Maybe one of her old teachers had taken the job this year. But why stare at her? Maybe she had imagined it. For years as a child she had daydreamed about Santa taking her to the North Pole and showing her where he made the toys.

The two middle school bands followed Santa, playing Christmas songs. They weren't bad. Every club in town marched in crooked rows. The 4-H club group reminded Anna of her years in it. Ms Marilyn's Dance School students danced and pranced, followed by war veterans in uniform waving flags. Bringing up the rear were the horses ridden by policemen in uniform. The old excitement she'd always felt filled her so much she knew she'd return for this next year and the next. Watching parades on television or in a crowd of thousands couldn't compare with this excitement.

When the parade ended Anna and her family bought hot dogs and moved from booth to booth at the end of the street. People waved to Anna and her parents. A few stopped to speak. Some asked about her life in Birmingham. A few asked if she had returned to say. All asked about her daddy's health. Of course everyone knew everyone's business. This was still a small town.

They went home for Daddy and Bella to take naps. It was difficult to determine who complained the most about leaving. Bella fell asleep on the way home. Anna took her upstairs and put her in the princess bed.

Daddy dozed on the sofa when they got home.

In the kitchen Anna and her mama sat with glasses of iced tea at the table. "Is Daddy worse than he admits? He looks tired, but he says he's fine.

Mama patted her hand. "The doctor arranged for tests. He didn't insist on putting your daddy in the hospital, so we figure he isn't worried. Doc suggested we cut down his fat intake and not do stressful things until we find out what's wrong. Daddy hasn't shown the usual heart attack symptoms. I just didn't think we needed to make the trip to your place until we could be sure. We didn't mean frighten you, honey.

Anna stirred the ice in her glass with a forefinger. "I know. But since I'm an adult and a mama, I need to be more considerate of my parents."

"Your aunts and cousins loved meeting Bella and seeing you again." Mama patted the hand that wasn't stirring.

"You're right. Bella got a kick out of them, too."

"Bella would love the Christmas tree lighting tonight. Come with us?" Her mama looked so much like Bella did when she begged.

Bella rose from her chair and hugged her. "Oh, Mama, I didn't even think about how much you and Daddy missed by spending the Friday and Saturday after Thanksgiving with me."

"Baby, we had already seen the local festivities for eighteen years. We loved being with our daughter and grandchild more!"

"Okay, we'll come with you. Bella will love it."

"Hello, hello," Aunt Jo-Jo called as she opened the backdoor and stuck her head inside. "Who's goin' to the tree lightin'?"

"We're all goin'."

"We plan to be there early and save space. I've got enough blankets to make space for the entire family. "

Anna remembered all the years she had complained about having to go to the lighting and sit with family instead of her friends. Her senior year in high school she'd had no idea she'd miss the next year because she would be very pregnant and living in a different state. She had begged to be allowed to go with John-Paul and friends. "But, Mama," she'd insisted. "I'll be with the kids from church."

Mama had said no. Would Bella insist she needed time away? Indeed, she would. That child had a stubborn, independent streak a mile long.

She startled when Aunt Jo-Jo hugged her.

"See you there?" Anna hadn't heard her aunt talking.

"Sure." She hugged Jo-Jo back. She had lived with Aunt Melly and loved the way she had grown closer to her, but she'd missed her other aunts, too.

Aunt Jo-Jo whispered, "Thinking about a boyfriend?"

Anna flushed at how close she'd come to guessing the truth. "No, ma'am. I was remembering how much I complained about having to go to every event with family instead of friends."

Her aunt laughed her belly laugh. "Your parents wanted to go prom with you, but I convinced 'em it wouldn't be a good idea."

"That is not true, " Mama said. "Your daddy and I offered to chaperone, that was all. "

"Mama, no." Anna gaped at her. "You didn't!" It might have been better for her if they had been there, embarrassing but better.

Aunt Jo-Jo left as quickly as she'd entered. Aunt

Marla and Aunt Melly breezed into the kitchen door so quickly they had surely meet Jo-Jo on the way in. Melly was staying with Marla until Monday and the news about Daddy. Aunt Marla hugged Anna and Mama on her way to the den to check on her brother. She came back into the room with Bella in her arms.

"This little one was sitting on her grandpa's lap, watching him snore."

Bella wrinkled her little nose. "Grandpa sores loud and his breath smells funny." She kissed Marla's cheek and reached for her mama.

Marla laughed. "He always did snore loudly. He must have eaten something that didn't smell good. "

Granny laughed. "Yes, he does snore, but he denies it, except when I push the record button on my phone and then play it back for him."

Anna rubbed noses with Bella and laughed. "Did you sleep well?"

Bella gave her a glare. "You put me in the little bed while I was sleepin'."

"Yes, I did. I didn't plan to take a nap and Granny got that bed just for you. "

"Okay, just for naps." An equal opportunity smoozer, Anna hugged every great aunt in the room before she wanted down to get on her kitchen throne.

***

Anne's family had joined other families who had staked out space on the grounds on the side of the courthouse square with the best views of the gigantic tree loaded with strings of lights waiting to be lit. Strings of white lights wound around tree trunks and limbs and light poles turned the courthouse grounds into a fairyland. Blankets covered almost every square inch of space not sidewalk. Several older folks had brought chairs to sit on parts of the concrete. The old excitement Anna had forgotten made her feel like a kid again.

Christmas carols played over loud speakers, but Bella seemed distracted by the living manger scene across the street in front of the First Baptist Church, the only Baptist church in the city limits. Apparently no one from outside had found the nerve to try to prevent the religious symbols from being displayed. It was on church property, of course. When Cousin Ben offered to take Bella to see it, she clapped her hands and danced around in circles, catching a few feet and making everyone laugh. Ben squatted and Anne helped Bella sit on the boy's broadening shoulders. Bella looked adorable with her sparkling Santa hat. Anna pulled her smartphone from her pocket and snapped photos for which he and Bella posed like pros. She peaked through Ben's reindeer antlers and grinned. He was only thirteen when she'd left. Now he'd filled out enough to be a halfback with a football scholarship to UGA. Bella giggled when he started striding and weaving around people on blankets.

Anna's family occupied four blankets grouped together. Everyone laughed and talked about tree lightings of the past, and again Anna regretted the ones she and her parents had missed. Well, no more.

Bella and Ben returned in time to take their places on a blanket for the tree lighting countdown. Mayor Stone stood on a platform beside the tree. He welcomed everyone and began the countdown with ten. Voices joined on nine and by eight everyone, including Bella, called out. With seven a shiver ran down Anna's spine. By the time they reached zero the tree blazed like it belonged on a Christmas card.

Bella's eyes sparkled when she turned to her mama. "It's be-u-ti-ful!"

And it was.

"Want to see Santa?" Ben asked Bella.

"Yes!" Bella tugged on Anna's hand. "Puleeze! Ma-ma! Can I?"

"I can take her," Ben offered.

"Mama, mama, mama, say yes! Please, please, please!

"Where?"

Ben pointed toward a space near the Courthouse steps.

Like magic, a fake snow-covered stage held a throne-like chair and a plump man in a red Santa suit. That had been added while she was gone. Weaving between blankets, Ben carried Bella piggyback this time. Lagging behind, she watched girls wave at Ben. That boy was using Bella as a babe magnet. Smart boy! She didn't want to cramp his style.

By the time then reached the Santa throne other children waited in line. The kid at the end of the line turned to Ben and looked up to his face. "You're too big to sit on Santa's lap."

Ben turned and squatted so Bella could slide to the ground. "I'm not," she said. She put her hands at her waist and glared at the boy. The boy who looked at least eight glared back at Bella and then shrugged. He turned around and moved forward in the line.

Anna walked beside the line while Ben talked to the girls who'd brought the younger brothers and sisters to see Santa. The closer they came to Santa, the more something seemed odd about him. Santa was a younger man with added stuffing. When Bella climbed up to Santa, Anna snapped a shot, expecting rebellion from Bella. Santa patted his knee and did a deep "Ho, ho, ho."

Bella stared at Santa and then grinned when he lifted her onto his knee. Anna's breath caught. Her daughter had balked each other time she'd been next in line to see the other Santas. But something else bothered Anna. Behind Santa's wire framed glasses eyes the same shade of green as Bella's twinkled. No way. Anna's heart skipped a beat. She had to be seeing things. She felt like Jonah when he learned he could run but not hide. When Bella stretched up to whisper in Santa's ear Anna caught her breath. When the child kissed Santa on his bearded cheek Anna's heart stopped for seconds.

Bella jumped down and ran to Anna. Excitement bubbling over, Bella listed the things Santa would bring her. "I told Santa a secret."

"I saw that." Anna glanced up at Santa. He stared at her instead of the little boy in his lap. *Oh, God. He knows.*

The rest of the evening Anna waited to hear from John Paul. She wouldn't go to him! She couldn't go to him!

When her parents headed to Sunday services Anna stayed home. Preacher and his wife would probably zone onto Bella, even in a crown of thousands or the few hundred there were likely in attendance.

Anna and Bella prepared their favorite meal for the family. They roasted corn on the cob and baking potatoes.

They wrapped cut veggies and potatoes with spices and grilled them in foil. Hamburgers waited for Daddy to grill. No turkey or ham for today.

Bella grabbed Christmas decorations from the box waiting for the formal decorating session planned for after lunch and put them on glass table on the screened in porch. The temperature was perfect. Her apartment didn't have a porch, so Anna figured they might as well enjoy this one.

She heard the garage door close and then the car doors. Each sound brought them closer to the usual discussion about who was at church, and who wore what, and who looked terrible because... and the sermon. Preacher had likely talked about honesty and Jonah.

Mama walked into the kitchen saying, "He didn't look good at all."

"Who didn't look good?" Bella piped up.

"Bella!" Anna scolded. "Granny wasn't talking to you, Nosey Rosie."

"Preacher," Mama answered.

"I'll change clothes and fire up the grill." Daddy kissed Anna's cheek and squatted to kiss Bella.

She kissed his smooth cheek with a loud smack and a giggle. "Your face isn't fuzzy like Santa's. I had to hunt for a place to kiss him."

Anna's parents stared at her, clearly interested. Silence hung in the air.

"When was this?" they asked as one voice.

"Last night when I told him a secret wish." Bella spread her arms with her hands palms up. She grabbed her grandpa's hand. "Go change your clothes so you can cook the hamburgers. I'm so hon-gry ----"

"Don't say it," Anna warned.

Anna tilted her head and raised one eyebrow. "I." She paused.

"Bella, " Anna warned.

"Could..."

"Your iPad could hide," Anna warned.

"Eat a .... lot!" Bella giggled and danced around.

"On that note, I'll go change." Daddy left the room laughing.

Everyone enjoyed the lunch.

When her daddy started to move boxes of decorations, Anna and her mother stopped him. Mama glared at him and helped Anna.

"Daddy, did you move that tree in here?" Anna stood with her hands on her hips.

"No, Sugar Pie, your cousin Ben came by and moved

all this stuff while you and Bella were outside workin' off lunch."

Bella giggled. "Workin' off our lunch?"

"He meant playing."

"Oh, I like workin' off our lunch!"

While Anna and her mama stood on matching ladders and started at the top of the eight-foot fake spruce tree and wound strings of lights around the tree, Bella but the balls and decorations in groups by color.

Aunt Jo-Jo stopped by and brought glasses of iced tea for the workers. "Got my tree done already. Come by and see it tomorrow."

"Maybe after Daddy's tests." Anna took a swallow of the tea, then put her glass on the coffee table in the one spot Bella had left clear.

"Why don't you bring Bella by my house on the way so you can stay with your mama?"

"Thank you!" Anna hugged her aunt.

By the time every decoration hung on the tree Bella was exhausted and happy. "Will Santa come see us here this Christmas or to our 'partment?"

"He will be where we are."

"I want him to come here." Bella stuck her little chin.

"We'll see."

Though they headed to bed early, Anna was sure no one would sleep well, but Bella. She didn't even bother to try to persuade her baby she could sleep in her little bed. Bella slept like the innocent. Anna tossed and turned. When her alarm went off at seven she had been dozing an hour. She knew this because she had watched the numbers move to six o'clock. This morning she didn't hit the snooze and turn over. By the time she had brushed her teeth and returned to the bedroom to grab some things for Bella to take to Aunt Jo Jo's and a change of clothes for the child and her, just in case, of course, Bella rolled over and reached for her. Watching her little one reach and root around for her made Anna smile. *God gave me that ray of sunshine.*

Bella lifted her head and looked around. Her sleepy smile when she spotted her mama warmed Anna's heart. "I'm goin' to Aunt Jo Jo's today?"

"Yes, you are."

"Yay!" Bella crawled from the bed and raced to the bathroom. She returned smelling like toothpaste and grinning. She grabbed the purple pants and wiggled into them. The tag on her purple and green sweatshirt showed when she pulled it over her head and down to her tummy. She pulled socks and tennis shoes on much more quickly than on days when she wasn't ready to meet a day. Maybe it was time for preschool for her instead of homeschooling her and with Aunt Melly.

***

Hours later Anna and her mama sat in a waiting room in the Medical Center, waiting for tests to end. Each had a paper cup of coffee machine sludge. Her mama raised her head at the sound of a masculine voice. Anna recognized it after five years, even though it sounded different without the help of the church sound system. A second, stronger, masculine voice brought Anna's head up. Preacher and John-Paul moved to the area where Anna's daddy had gone. Would John-Paul return here to wait with her soon? What would they talk about? Or would he even speak to her? He had to acknowledge her mama, but they hadn't parted company on not so good terms. He'd had good reason to believe she had found a new man as soon as she'd left him. Maybe there was another waiting room, or maybe Daddy would be in a room by the time her baby's daddy came back.

Fifteen minutes later John-Paul walked into the waiting room and hugged her mama. "I know your husband will be okay. He and Daddy have the same doctor. "

"Where's your mama?"

"She woke up with a fever, so we left her at home with her sister to take care of her. Daddy wanted to stay and look after her, but she laid down the law. We need to find out how sick he really is."

"I'll run by and check on her tomorrow."

"No, ma'am, you won't. You need to stay away from any sick folks so you can take care of your husband." He gave her a peck on the cheek the way he had when he and Anna dated.

He moved to her other side and sat down beside Anna. Her heart lodged in her throat. He took her left hand in his and turned it over, palm up. "I've missed you."

Words wouldn't come, but tears insisted on forming in Anna's eyes. She swallowed hard. Her lips trembled. She couldn't hide the truth. "I've missed you, too." Had he heard the story about a husband who had died?

There was a time when she'd have flung herself into his arms and let him hold her and reassure her everything would turn out all right. That had ended the minute she'd left to go to Alabama.

"You have a beautiful little girl. How old is she?" He used the soft voice that had always made her melt.

Her stomach flipped and her palms sweated. "Bella is four. "

"Where is her daddy?" His green eyes looked into hers.

She looked over his shoulder. There was no way she

could look into his eyes and lie. "Why do you ask?"

He touched a tear that rolled down her cheek. She flinched while she wished she could turn her check into his palm. He turned her face so she had to look into his eyes.

"She told Santa she wanted a daddy."

"Oh, God." Her throat ached with the pain of the lies she'd had to tell. Could she tell the lie again? "I can't do this!" She tried to pull away. The man she had loved for as long as she could remember held her face with his gentle hands on her cheeks.

"Is there something you need to tell me, Anna?"

There was a time when he'd called her darlin', and she wished with all her heart things could be like that again, but they couldn't. Too much stood between them. "You know?" Her voice shook.

"The moment I looked into Bella's eyes I thought I knew. When I lifted her onto my knee my heart knew she was my child."

"But---"

"Why didn't you tell me?" His gentle voice made her feel more guilty than she had ever felt before. She had kept his child from him for four years.

"We weren't ready for marriage. You had plans for college and seminary."

"What? I'd have given all of that up to be with you."

She touched his hands, hands she had adored and missed. If only she could have held them while she gave birth to their baby. "I couldn't let you do that. Your daddy would have insisted we marry. You would have married me because of guilt. I couldn't do that to you, to us."

"Of course I would have married you. I loved you."

"That was the point." Her voice sounded stronger than she felt at the moment. "I wasn't ready to let you take care of me. Though I loved you, I really didn't want to be a preacher's wife. I needed to grow up, and I did."

"Anna, I decided I didn't want to be a preacher. My parents wanted it for me. I figured that out while I was at Mercer. I still wanted you, though."

He swallowed so hard she saw his Adam's apple move twice. "If Daddy hadn't been so sick when I got home Saturday night and Sunday, I'd have been at your folks house with a hundred questions. I almost approached your parents at church, but Mama was so concerned about my dad. I want to be in my daughter's life. Santa can't break his promise to get her a daddy this Christmas."

"Won't your folks be upset to know you have a child?"

He shrugged. "They will be so excited about their grandchild they'll adjust."

She raised her eyebrows in disbelief.

"They love kids."

"They'll try to insist we marry."

"I'm a college graduate and I interviewed for a teaching job at Stoneridge high school to replace a math teacher. Her husband is being transferred to Texas in two weeks. I want to be here for my parents if Daddy needs by-pass surgery. I'm ready to be a father, and I can stand up for us and what we believe is right for us and Bella. We can make our own decisions. "

"Sweetie." Her mama's light touch and sweet voice reminded her she and John-Paul weren't the only people in the room. How could she have forgotten her own daddy was having a serious procedure she knew could be dangerous and her mama would be worrying. Anna turned to her and saw her relieved smile. "Your daddy's waiting in a room, and the nurse said he's fine. You stay here and keep John-Paul company. You have a lot of catching up to do."

"It's okay, I'll be at your house tomorrow afternoon to see my daughter."

Mama, bless her heart, pulled out her granny bragging book and handed it to him. "Keep it."

Anna touched his cheek and rose to leave. He stood and pulled her into his arms and kissed her with such gentleness she almost wept. "Go see your dad and let him know Bella has her daddy now. You and I can start over, and this time we'll be grownups."

Matt's Christmas Angel

Mary Marvella

"What am I going to do about Matt?" Guenivere Jones asked her mirror. "He's the nicest person I've ever known." Gwen brushed her long, auburn hair for the fiftieth stroke on her way to one hundred. Gwen had inherited G Granny's hair color, a tad too red for her taste.

Of course the mirror made no suggestions. It never did.

"He's thoughtful, he's kind, and he's not bad looking, either." Gwen sighed and shook the brush at her reflection.

G Granny insists he's my beau. She's even ordered her wedding dress cleaned and pressed for me to wear. But Matt and I aren't even dating. The white velvet gown had been altered for G. Granny, Grandma Mary, then for Felicia Guenivere, Gwen's mother.

"Stroke ninety-nine. I quit." Gwen stuck out her tongue at the mirror. "G. Granny, I'm not getting married this Christmas. Not to Matt, not to anybody, so you're wastin'

49

your time getting the dress ready. When the time's right I'll wear it, if I get married in the winter, like all you other Gueniveres have."

Gwen loved G. Granny. Everyone loved the matriarch, the reason every first daughter in the family had been named Guenivere for four generations. Her premonitions were legendary. Sharp as a tack, she had lived nearly one hundred years, but she was so-o-o-o wrong this time. If Gwen ever had a daughter, she would not name her Guenivere.

Matt was her best friend in the whole world. She adored him, but she wasn't in love with him.

Gwen slid into bed, ready for a good night's sleep. She and Matt had only twelve days to accomplish their twelve traditional Christmas missions. This Christmas would mark their twenty-fifth together as best friends. Gwen settled down into her nest of comforters and pillows. Ninety-nine strokes. No one does the one hundred brush stroke thing anymore. Hah!

***

Sleep captured Gwen in its gentle arms and eased her into her fondest memory. She was three years old and playing in her sandbox, the one mama said had been hers once upon a time. A child she'd never seen walked up to her sandbox and stood, staring at her.

"You Gwen?" The boy's face puckered up in a frown.

Gwen nodded slowly. "Uh huh. Who are you?"

The boy looked bigger than she was and real skinny. His glasses made him look like an owl. He carried a pail and a shovel. He had light, short hair.

"Matthew Henry Simmons," he said. He must be serious about the long name, because he wasn't smiling.

"This is my sandbox. Wanna play?"

"Sure." He still didn't smile.

Gwen grinned when she thought about his red plastic bucket and shovel. She remembered the gentleness of five-year old Matt. He had been her playmate ever since. That Christmas he had told her about the "Twelve Days of Christmas" song he'd learned in kindergarten. He'd also taught her to count to one hundred.

***

Matt's image faded.

"You forgot something, Gwen."

Gwen awoke as though she had actually heard the gentle accusation from G. Granny. So what would happen if she failed to do the one hundredth stroke? Who knew?

Some questions a woman shouldn't ask. Why argue with an old lady whose hair still looked lustrous and shiny as angel hair in her nineties? At 4 AM Gwen dragged out of her warm bed and grabbed the brush. One hundred. After that she slept until her alarm jarred her awake.

***

Excitement woke Gwen early Saturday morning. The aromas of baking yeast bread and bacon frying sent Gwen down to the kitchen, ready to fuel up for a busy day. Her excitement made finishing the eggs and bacon difficult, despite her grumbling stomach.

Mama passed around the tray of Christmas cinnamon bread. "G. Granny, would you care for more coffee?"

"No, thank you, dear. I never have more than one cup."

Gwen had heard that answer every time her mother or anyone else offered a second cup of coffee to the *Queen Mother*. Even at breakfast she looked regal in her high-necked blouse and cameo broach and earrings.

"Mama, more coffee?" Felicia asked Gram Mary.

"Just a little – to freshen this." She held her cup toward Felicia as Gwen watched the drama unfold as usual. "Thank you." She checked her watch as she did every morning. "Gotta finish this cup and head over to the church. Josiah wants one last solo practice before the *Messiah* performance tomorrow night." Gram had played the church organ for as long as Gwen could remember.

"Felicia," G. Granny asked. "could you take me shopping this morning? I believe our Gwen has special plans."

Gwen glanced at the lady who had ruined her sleep last night. "How did you know?" she asked.

The old woman smiled. "Your Matt's here to start your twelve missions," she answered. The front doorbell pealed Jingle Bells. "See?"

Instead of telling G. Granny he was not "her" Matt, Gwen glanced to the kitchen door-frame. *How does she do that?*

Gram Mary went to let Matt in, though no one would have minded if he had just walked in. Within seconds Matt strode into the kitchen, his hair still almost corn silk blond as the day she'd met him. His broad shoulders seemed to span the door opening. His brilliant blue eyes squinted at her.

Gram Mary carried his glasses, rubbing the foggy lenses with a cloth. She handed them to the smiling giant of a man who then hugged her. "Is your mama feeling better?" she asked.

"Yes, ma'am, she musta had a bug. She's fine this morning. I'll tell Mama you asked about her."

"Good." Gram Mary picked up her cup and took a last

sip of coffee. "Felicia, I'll meet you and mother for lunch at Macy's at Lenox Square," she said as she kissed Mama's cheek. "I can help you this afternoon if Felicia has things she needs to do." She hugged G. Granny.

"Have fun, you two," Gram whispered in Gwen's ear.

Gwen saw her grandmama wink at Matt before breezing from the kitchen.

"Good morning, Matthew," G. Granny said when he stopped at her chair to lean over and kiss her pale cheek. They smiled at each other as though they shared a secret.

Matt dwarfed Mama when he planted a kiss on her cheek.

"Coffee?"

At Matt's nod Mama filled his cup. "Care for a hunk of Christmas bread and some bacon?"

In her usual take-care-of-folks manner, Gwen had buttered a hunk of bread for Matt. He had never refused food in the twenty years she had known him. He didn't refuse this time. Nor did he mention that he could butter his own bread. He'd have done the same for her.

"Mornin', Gwen," he finally said.

"Mornin'." She handed Matt the bread.

Their hands touched as they had hundreds of times.

This time something felt different.

Matt's sky blues stared at her through his glasses. His gaze held hers. Her heart stuttered to a stop. Her lungs refused to work. Dropping her gaze lower didn't help. His generous mouth formed a smile bright enough to blind her. Gwen had to remember to swallow. How very strange!

A loud chuckle broke the spell caused by lack of sleep or the power of suggestion from one meddlesome old lady. Jerking her hand back as though he had burned it, Gwen stood so quickly she knocked her chair over. She leaned over to right it, but Matt reached a long arm down and beat her to it. "Thanks, I'll get my boots and join you for our errands in a jiffy, Matt. Have some bacon while I get ready."

Before he could say anything Gwen escaped upstairs to her room for her boots. Her reaction to Matt disturbed her. Surely G. Granny's predictions had put the idea into her head. Maybe she should've saved herself the sleepless night by simply brushing her hair the whole hundred strokes, as G. Granny always insisted. The woman could be downright spooky.

By the time Gwen returned downstairs she felt calm and in control. Matt was helping G. Granny with her coat. He wound her scarf on her white head and around her neck. He always treated the women in her family with care, especially G. Granny. Mama wore her coat and gloves. She and G.

Granny left to tend to errands.

Within seconds Gwen and Matt stood alone beside the entry closet. When she reached inside to get her jacket, he reached past her to grab it.

Matt held her jacket, as he had many times. Gwen trembled inside, as she never had with Matt or any other man. His hands lingered at her neck and pulled her hair from under the collar after he settled the garment on her shoulders. When he placed his strong hands on her shoulders she turned to face him, as she had many times before. Her heart raced peculiarly when he zipped her jacket under her chin. He was her best friend and she must be imagining things had changed between them. When he touched her cheek with a callused finger she sighed.

When he released her so he could get his own jacket she gathered her supplies. Today they would complete their first mission, cutting Christmas trees to give away.

***

The drive from Stone Mountain to Dahlonega passed quietly with Christmas Carols playing on the CD she'd made for Matt years ago when they were in high school. She'd had little money to spare. It almost matched the one she kept in her own car, the one Matt made for her that same year, his senior year.

"So, how will the office get by without you there for

two weeks?" she asked. "Jason complained like a kid when I reminded him I wouldn't be at work until after Christmas. You'd think he had forgotten I do this every year."

"They must miss you at the bookstore. I finished all my cases with a day to spare, so no court for me this week. I won't miss driving around Atlanta with all the shopping traffic." Matt glanced at her. "I do miss being here to enjoy the small pleasures of our little village and being able to see you every day."

"I miss not seeing you, too, but you're doin' the right thing. Besides, we see each other when you visit your folks. Being able to text helps, too, like coordinating our twelve deeds for this Christmas. I found two houses for us to repair and rounded up a crew of volunteers for tomorrow afternoon and Monday. The lumberyard will supply anything we need. Miz Luce and Maryanne Stuart haven't been able to do anything to their houses since Luce's son died and Maryanne's husband abandoned her."

"Excellent choices, Gwen, I'm already searching for Maryanne's no account husband, and I'll see he pays for abandoning her and the kids."

In the lull that followed anticipation hung in the air of the truck cab. Gwen glanced at Matt, who looked serious.

"I've been thinking of opening an office in the old Village and renting out my condo in midtown." He didn't turn from the road to check her reaction.

"That sounds great." At least she thought it did. How would seeing him every day affect their relationship?

An hour later Matt led the way to the wooded area near the house that belonged to G. Granny. She wasn't strong enough to care for the old house, which was too far from any neighbors to suit her family and her doctors. She'd neared her eightieth birthday when she'd become Gwen's live-in baby sitter and the self-proclaimed best cook in the large house Gwen's father had built. She'd chosen that groom as she had all the girls' husbands. And now she'd chosen Matt. She'd bequeathed the farmhouse and land to Gwen instead of her daughter or granddaughter.

Gwen helped Matt chop down twelve spruce trees from the forest started by Great Granddad at G. Granny's request. Hired farmhands replenished the trees each year and kept the house and barns repaired. Great Granddad had taught Matt how to choose the trees to harvest. Matt and Gwen dragged the trees to Matt's Ford muscle truck and loaded them. Their first harvest many years ago had included much smaller trees, but they had been so proud of their bounty and so excited to share.

Matt and Gwen delivered each tree to a place they had selected earlier. One went to a small free clinic, four to small churches with low budgets. The women's shelter and the homeless shelter were next in line. The other six went to poorer families with children. By suppertime Gwen wanted to collapse and put her feet up after a long hot shower. Her desk job wasn't keeping her in shape.

She trudged up the steps to her front porch, with Matt's hand on her back. Standing on the porch, Gwen huddled against his broad body to escape the wind instead of opening her door to go inside. Snuggling inside his coat, she took a deep breath of his woodsy scent. His truck had been warm, but evening had brought out the cold the sun had held at bay all day.

Matt had smiled when she'd invited him to stay for supper, but he'd declined since his folks expected him. "Mama needs for me to move some heavy furniture around to get out our decorations." Matt smiled down at Gwen. "Daddy has to watch his back so his won't be laid up for Christmas again."

"Say hey to your folks for me. See you tomorrow." Reluctant, Gwen pushed away from the warmth to go inside.

"Gwen." Matt's voice sounded odd.

She looked up to see what bothered him.

He glanced overhead.

She followed his gaze and spotted the gigantic bunch of mistletoe tied to the porch support. Someone had arranged it in a place impossible to miss.

Her best friend looked into her eyes. His head blocked the light, making his long-lashed blue eyes difficult to see. His chocolate-minty breath warmed her face. Her gaze moved to Matt's beautiful mouth. He was going to kiss her as he had many times before. No big deal.

His lips grazed one corner of her mouth. She shivered. He kissed the other side. Her own lips parted slightly. He had never kissed her like this before. The kiss deepened. She had never kissed him back like this before. When the kiss ended Matt had to guide her to the door and push her inside. She touched her lips with trembling fingers, still tasting Matt and chocolate mint candy. A very big deal! Should she strangle the person who had placed the mistletoe there or hug her? Surely one of the grands had done it!

***

Gwen remembered little about what she ate for supper, since her mind stayed occupied with memories of a kiss that had curled her toes and stolen her brain. She noticed the women in her family staring at her on occasion, but she was too bewildered to dwell on it. She remembered little about bed preparations. She did remember brushing her hair. She was too tired for the required one hundred strokes, but each time she thought she would stop she remembered getting out of bed to stroke that last time last night. After stoke one hundred she dropped the pearl-handled gift G. Granny had given her for her twelfth birthday.

Crawling into her bed, Gwen settled into the warmth of the electric blanket her mother had set on low earlier. Matt could have made the blanket unnecessary. For seconds Gwen imagined cuddling up to his big body. They'd kept each other warm on campouts years ago and sat on the front porch swing sharing blankets and counting the stars on chilly evenings. The heady warmth Gwen imagined all night in her dreams was a different matter altogether.

***

Breakfast the next four mornings was the same as most but different. Everyone seemed to be staring at Gwen and smirking. Even her father, whose morning appointments at the hospital began late, for a change, seemed in on a secret.

She tried to avoid touching Matt or looking into his eyes, or at his mouth, or at his broad shoulders or superb, muscular chest. She failed, of course, since they worked so closely together and he was so handsome.

For mission six they headed to the homeless shelter for the day. Muscles strained for the last two days while they cleaned yards, mended steps, replaced doors and even five windows, and painted walls inside and out groaned. They had left two families in warm homes, thanks to donations from Stone Mountain Hardware Store and a crew of ten people. All day at the shelter Matt and Gwen washed and scrubbed pots and pans and served food. They laundered bedding and threadbare blankets and added new ones to the shelter's supply. Matt had brought extras so people could take one when they left. They scrubbed floors and watched small restless children so their parents could rest without wondering what the kids were getting into.

When everyone had been fed Matt insisted Gwen sit down and rest for a few minutes. Neither had eaten, so they strolled outside and found a bench sheltered by a wall. He pulled two sandwiches from a bag Gram had brought by for them earlier and set them in front of Gwen. She watched Matt open two Coke Zeros. After a long swallow of his drink he moved beside her. She was so tired she couldn't move.

"Gwen, sweetheart, you gotta eat." He held a sandwich to her lips. "Come on, take a nice, big bite. Come on." His usually deep voice had a sing song quality, like the one he used for children. He moved the sandwich around, making silly sounds. "Here it comes."

She smiled at his antics, then she opened her mouth and took a bite before he started making flying motions. He patiently held the can for her to drink when she had swallowed the first bite. She took the sandwich from him and bit into its goodness. Fresh homemade bread, sliced ham, and tomato slices made her taste buds explode. "Now you eat."

By the time she'd finished her sandwich she felt revived. When he dug in the bag and brought out a Hershey's Dark Chocolate bar she grabbed for it. He held it over head and unwrapped it.

"Stay still and I'll share," he promised.

Gwen stilled and waited. *He'd better share.*

He did. Matt held a large piece for her to bite. One broad hand held both of hers still, so she couldn't grab it. Once she bit he swooped in and bit the same piece from the other end. His warm, moist lips grazed hers. He didn't exactly kiss her. What he did was more erotic when their lips touched in the middle of the chocolate bar.

***

All night Gwen tossed and turned. She'd expected Matt to kiss her goodnight, but her father had opened the door just as Matt was leaning down toward her. All night she lived that anticipated kiss over and over again in her dreams. Why was kissing Matt different this time? Had he ever kissed her lips before this week? Of course he had, but not the same way. He had never made her want to kiss him back and hang on to him for dear life. Her recent fascination with her best friend puzzled her. He had her stomach tied in knots, her brain scrambled, and her hormones raging.

***

Mission seven made Gwen happy when she and Matt walked into the rented space on Main Street where they collected toys and nonperishable food. For days someone in his family or hers had opened the shop and collected toys and clothes and personal grooming products. Today Matt organized the donations while she distributed them as people came in.

Sadly, some of the same people Gwen had seen last year and the year before were still in need this year. They also gave out certificates for free haircuts at the barber shop down the street and gift certificates for McDonald's. The restaurants of Stone Mountain proved their generosity by supplying hot coffee and hot chocolate and wrapped sandwiches people could take with them. Someone had brought bags of apples, oranges, and bananas last night. It broke Gwen's heart to know that some of the folks who left here with food and clothes might go hungry and kids would have no Christmas without the help she and Matt and their families provided. The soup kitchen and churches couldn't provide enough hot meals to feed everyone who had fallen on hard times. When school was in session some kids got hot lunches, at least.

When people stopped coming to the makeshift store,

Matt and Gwen finished in time to stroll to the ART Station to enjoy a performance of *A Broadway Christmas Carol*. Sitting in the Cabaret Bar, they gazed into each other's eyes.

Nancy Knight stopped by. "Hello, are you enjoying the show?"

"Oh, yes." Matt nodded and shook her hand.

"I love what you've done with this area. And the trains are a lovely touch!" Gwen said. She couldn't have told anyone the name of the woman who played the piano or what she played. She was too busy looking at Matt. Her grandma Mary would say she was smitten. How had she missed the love in Matt's eyes over the years? When had their friendship become so much more?

***

Sunday morning started the same way the other mornings had. As she buttered Matt's Christmas bread she wondered if she could avoid the intimacy of touching hands when she gave it to him.

He took the lead and guided her hand to his mouth. When he took one huge bite his lips grazed her fingers, but he didn't turn her hand loose. *So much for wanting to escape the snare of Matt's look and the magic in his touch!*

She gulped. Watching him chew mesmerized her. She knew how his mouth felt against hers, and she wanted to feel it again.

The buzzing in her ears drowned out all sound around them. They might as well have been alone. Each bite he took pulled her closer to him. He took the last bite from her fingers and put it into her mouth.

A chair scraped. The buzzing stopped. Her voice seemed loud to her own ears. "Time to head out to the women's shelter," she said.

Matt held her chair. He helped her into her coat, taking extra pains to make sure it lay smoothly on her shoulders. When they walked to his truck parked in her driveway his large hand rested on her back. He handed her up into his truck with care that seemed almost intimate. All the way to the old converted church building just inside the city limits of Stone Mountain Village he held her enthralled while he detailed his suggestions for the rest of the deeds for the week.

The tree they had delivered earlier now held homemade decorations. It was so beautiful and so sad. These women and their children had nowhere else to go and needed the temporary support of the congregation which met now in a brand new building two miles down the road. This church housed only mothers with small children.

Gwen and Matt toted stacks of brightly wrapped boxes they had collected as donations at the building Matt's dad owned. At least there would be gifts for the people who stayed here until Christmas.

G. Granny's gingerbread and molasses cookies were a hit. Gram's hand-knitted gloves would warm these children, and personalized books Mama had made on her computer would thrill them. Mama had stayed up all night making sure she had a book for each child there as of the day before.

Gwen thought about how blessed she was to have her wonderful family. She noticed a new little girl huddled in a corner. The child shivered as if from fear. The oversized sweater didn't seem to warm her enough. Matt stood nearby. His voice had a gentle tone as he knelt, making himself closer to her height.

"Hi," he said. His voice was so soft Gwen had to strain to hear him. "I'm Matt and this is my friend Gwen. Do you have a name?"

The child's silence spoke her fear. She shook her head.

Matt looked thoughtful, then he smiled. "Well, we'll just have to give you a name. Shall we call you Princess Drucilla?"

She frowned at Matt as if to say that wasn't her name.

A thin woman inched closer to Matt, ready to protect

her baby.

Matt sat on the floor. He looked to the other children standing in a group, watching the scene.

One by one each child walked over to Matt and hugged him. Each looked at the frightened girl and told her that Mr. Matt was a good guy.

"He's our friend," a tiny girl with short brown hair said in her sweet voice.

"He won't hurt us." A boy who looked to be six nodded.

"We love Mr. Matt." The tiny girl had been leery about his size just a month ago when he'd taken the mothers and children to Stone Mountain Park in a rented bus.

"He's with our Princess Guenivere." A third munchkin joined the chorus of reassuring children.

"She's new here, she'll get used to you, Mr. Matt." The oldest child in the bunch patted Matt's arm, looking old for his ten years. "Her name's Becky."

Matt said solemnly, "Well, if I had a little girl I would treat her like a princess. I'd never hurt her."

Becky had moved a step from the corner. "What if you had a little boy?" she whispered.

"He'd be my best buddy," Matt answered. "next to my

other best buddy." He looked at Gwen and smiled.

His blue eyes were so misty looking at him made Gwen's throat tighten. She nodded. "He's my best friend, too," she said.

The frightened child stepped closer. "Do you want a little girl?" she asked.

"More than just about anything in the world." Matt's voice was gravelly and hoarse and he looked as though he meant it.

Gwen's heart swelled. Neither had ever mentioned wanting children, but she did, she realized. Or she would someday in the future. Had some man not wanted this beautiful child to be his?

Matt held out his hand palm up. In it lay a small white object. "Would you like to share my Christmas Angel?"

A tear rolled down Gwen's cheek as Becky took a step closer to Matt, close enough to touch his fingertips.

"Would you like to hold her?" he asked. "I made her, like I made the other little carvings I gave everyone."

Leaning forward, Becky reached to take the angel from Matt's hand. She took one step back but didn't retreat into her corner. The wounded animal look had gone. Her eyes misted as she rubbed a dirty finger over the piece of wood. She glanced up at Gwen. "She looks like you. You must be his Christmas Angel." Her voice sounded stronger. She looked back at Matt. "Is she?"

Matt nodded and looked at Gwen. "I hope so, dear God, I hope so." His love shone in his eyes as he looked back at Gwen.

Gwen nodded at the beautiful, gentle man. Her throat ached with the words bubbling up from her heart. "I'll be your Christmas Angel. You're my Christmas Angel, too." Someone sniffed.

Becky looked at her mother, who had lost some of her haggard look. When her mother nodded, Becky stepped forward and hugged Matt. "Thank you, Mr. Matt." She kissed his cheek.

"Thank you, Princess Becky." Matt stood slowly with Gwen's help. He took her in his strong arms. "So, when are you going to give us a little girl or boy to spoil?" he asked. "I want lots of little Christmas Angels."

"Don't you think we ought to get married first?" Gwen smiled up at her Matt. She had loved this man forever, but never as much as she did at this moment. "We might better tell the family, too."

"Thought you'd never ask, Angel. They all already know. The winter-white, velvet wedding gown has been cleaned and pressed. Granny G said it should be a perfect fit for you now."

"I knew something was going on." Gwen laughed. "That woman!"

"Granny asked preacher if we could be married at the church on Christmas Day. He said yes." Matt looked up at a sprig of mistletoe above. He lifted Gwen's chin with one finger, then he kissed her. He rubbed his lips against hers. He parted his lips and kissed her fully, deeply.

The kiss went on and on, even after the clapping and childish giggles started. The kids seemed to like the kissing, though they were a tad young to be watching this. Maybe it would help them believe in love that doesn't hurt.

When Gwen finally came up for air she asked, "What about a license, a wedding party, a reception?"

"We have to finish signing for the license and get blood tests tomorrow. It's all arranged. Your cousins and mine will all be here in Stone Mountain for our Christmas wedding."

"Pretty sure of yourself, weren't you?"

"I've planned this since we met at your sandbox, and G. Granny said she started planning earlier."

That chilly evening Gwen and Matt strolled hand-in-hand to see the live nativity scene on the lawn of the First Baptist Church. The beauty of the Christmas story never failed to make Gwen teary and happy. Matt held her close to his warmth, and she snuggled in.

***

Sunday dawned cold and clear. Matt arrived to take Gwen to visit at the assisted living home where they visited with older folks and entertained them. Gwen played the piano while Matt sang Christmas carols in his rich baritone. They helped serve lunch of turkey and dressing and all the fixin's. Gwen thanked The Good Lord that G. Granny had her family to take care of her. Still sharp and healthy, the sassy old lady showed no signs of slowing down any time soon.

Matt's gentleness with each person there made Gwen's heart swell with pride. Old men shook his hand and women hugged him. One even made her laugh by grabbing his firm butt.

"Looked like the women liked you." Gwen grinned as they left.

"You made a lot of men smile, yourself." Matt's squeeze made Gwen giggle like a teenager.

"I've never been pinched so many times in my life." She laughed.

***

Gwen couldn't stop looking at Matt, who grinned all the way to the courthouse in Decatur. She couldn't believe that in only three days he would be her husband. They pointed out Christmas Decorations they remembered from years past. Filling out the paperwork happened in a blur with lots of laughing by each of them.

Soon Matt stopped at the Georgia Power office on Memorial Drive and produced a list of twelve names. The startled clerk raised her penciled eyebrows and glared at Matt and Gwen over the wire rimmed glasses perched so far on her nose they looked ready to fall off.

"Can I help you?" Her voice sounded nasal and she looked like she didn't want to be working.

"We'd like to pay these bills." He passed the list through an opening in the protective glass barrier. She looked at the paper as though it might bite her. Beside each name he had written the account numbers. He waited patiently while she got up and went through a door in the back of the office and then returned with an older woman Gwen recognized.

"Matt, good to see you again," the older woman chirped.

"Miz Lila, good to see you, too. Mama told me to wish you a Merry Christmas and give you this." He handed her a folded card. Then he held Gwen's left hand out so the engagement ring sparkled, despite the dull light. You must come to the wedding Wednesday evening."

Gwen grinned as Miz Lila and the puzzled clerk admired the antique white-gold ring. Matt turned on his lazy grin and took out a wad of twenty dollar bills. The women entered each name into the computer and told Matt how much that person owed. He counted out twenty dollar bills and paid each in turn. He had brought just enough, since he had checked to see how much money he would need. By the time he and Gwen called out "Merry Christmas" and left, the new clerk looked at Matt with the same adoration most women showed.

Gwen just hugged him hard and laughed. Hugging Matt had taken on a new personality. He made her feel safe and adored. And she planned to hug him often until they were old and gray.

***

On Tuesday John Bass and Sarah Temple waited in the large room with neatly folded clothes and shelves of food still to be distributed to folks in need. Sarah huddled in silence, keeping an eye on her shopping cart filled with trash bags, while John paced, muttering. "They ain't gonna come. I know they ain't."

The time Matt spent arranging a place for John to shower and shave had made a change in the way he carried himself. The fresh haircut made him look ten years younger. The second hand suit and dress shirt made him look almost

74

like he was ready for church or a business meeting.

Gwen's stomach lurched with fear the old man was right and poor John would fall deeper into depression. He didn't need any more disappointments. "Your sons said they were grateful to get your letter when they called Matt yesterday, and they will be here soon."

Noise outside the door made her look up at the store front window and stopped John in his tracks.

Two tall men and three women exited an older model Bronco. The way they talked and gestured showed their excitement and anticipation.

"I can't believe we finally found Daddy," a woman's feminine voice said. She looked up and down the street, as though she might find him.

"Yes." One of the well-dressed men looked at a card and checked the address over the door. "This is the right place. We are to meet Dad here. Come on, let's go inside."

John stood rooted to his spot. He twisted the dirty cap he hadn't let them put into his trash bag of possessions.

Gwen ached for him. Her stomach felt as empty as if she had skipped breakfast and as shaky.

The women hurried in while a man held the door open and paused for a second, surveying the room. The second one of them spotted John. She and the others lunged toward him, enveloping him, laughing and crying.

"Daddy, we finally found you!"

"Oh, my God!"

"Thank the Good Lord."

Gwen and Sarah let their tears flow at the sight. These women loved John, though he'd been afraid they wouldn't want him in their lives.

The men who looked like John strode to join the women and hugged him, dwarfing him.

All the hugging made Gwen feel better. Ten minutes later when Matt came through the front door everyone turned to him and then noticed Gwen and Sarah were in the room. John made introductions all around. Matt suggested they all go next door for lunch and talk, but John's family wanted to take him home immediately. Gwen handed John a card and reminded his family they should return to see his counselor in a week.

"We'll bring him back, but we want him with us for Christmas so he'll know how much we love him." The taller man shook hands with Gwen, Matt, and even Sarah, who tried to stay in the background, before handing Gwen an envelope. John hugged Gwen and Matt before he let his family usher him out the door to a new life.

"Be right back." Sarah's disappointment showed

despite her smiles the whole time John's family hugged him and led him out to their vehicle. Her shoulders slumped and she began to rearrange the bags in her cart as though she believed she would need them tonight.

"Stay and have a cup of coffee and a sandwich." Gwen couldn't let Sarah give up and leave. Her sister had promised she'd come this afternoon. Turning, Gwen grabbed a cup and poured coffee into it.

"Sarah?" the voice made Gwen turn around.

"Beth?" Sarah sobbed.

A slender woman reached up and hesitantly touched Sarah's face, like she needed to prove that Sarah was real. The tears running down both women's cheeks made Gwen tear up again. She gulped around the lump in her throat.

"I missed you," the smaller woman said as she hugged Sarah.

"I missed you, too." Sarah hugged back.

"Come home with me."

"I can't. I did things." Sarah turned away.

"I don't care. I need you. Do you want me to join you here on the streets? I will if you don't come home and let me help you. If you aren't happy being at home, I'll bring you back. At least stay for a week."

Yes, give it a try, please. Gwen held her breath, waiting for Sarah's response, praying she would spend Christmas with family.

"Okay, I will."

Matt returned from outside and grinned at Gwen. "Her sister was lost and I sent her here. Poor woman forgot her glasses and couldn't read the address in the letter I sent her."

"Good job!"

Matt stepped forward. "Need help with your things, Sarah?"

Sarah's sister released her long enough to offer her hand to him. "Maggie Scott. I assume you are Matt?"

"Yes, ma'am, I am, and that's Gwen by the coffee pot on the counter."

Gwen moved close enough to shake hands with Maggie, whose cinnamon and vanilla scent made Gwen smile. Sarah would enjoy being with this down-to-earth woman who had baked before she came to get her sister. Maggie would enjoy home cooked meals for a change.

"Thank you so much for taking care of my sister." Maggie hugged Gwen and then Matt.

Sarah hugged Gwen so long Gwen wondered if she had changed her mind about leaving. She had been living on the streets here for at least three years. Maybe the thing that made her run worried her still.

Matt gave a card to Maggie. "Make sure she gets back to see her counselor the week after Christmas." Matt grabbed the garbage bags of Sarah's belongings and nodded to Sarah and Maggie. Matt held the door open so the ladies could pass.

Gwen took steps toward the door and street-front window to watch Matt handle Sarah's meager belongings with care as he put the bags in the back seat of a recent model Lexus.

Sarah hugged him and then got into the car. Matt shut her door and stood in the street, watching the car disappear.

***

Christmas evening people packed the church to capacity. Vans had brought people from the homeless shelter and from the women's shelter, so every pew was filled. Christmas bells and candles covered every flat surface, and stars hung on the walls. The tree glittered with twinkling lights like so many stars when lights in the sanctuary dimmed. The choir sang "Joy to the World" while three tuxedo-clad man escorted G. Granny, Gram Mary, and Gwen's mama down the aisle to their pew. Matt's brother escorted his Mama to her pew as the last note sounded.

Gwen waited in the vestibule with her daddy. She was

79

so very ready to spend her wedding night at the Stone Mountain Inn and her honeymoon at the family tree farm. There was no better place to begin their life together.

Her photographer, Danielle Jarrell, snapped shots of Gwen and her daddy and of Madeline Quick, Gwen's best friend, arranging the heavy velvet train attached to the wedding gown. By the time Maid of Honor, Madeline, headed down the aisle, Gwen's heart beat so hard she could barely breathe. She and her daddy stepped into the doorway of the sanctuary.

She trembled at the sight of Matt in his black tux. She had never seen any man so handsome. And he was her Christmas present for life. The aisle seemed to be mile long as the wedding march and the sight of Matt at the altar with the minister drew her like a magnet. The man she needed in her world forever waited for her with a look of love and awe.

The ceremony passed in a blur. Matt repeated the minister's words in a strong voice. Her voice trembled with emotion when she said her own vows. Her heart filled with more love than she had thought possible.

When the minister pronounced them husband and wife, she grabbed Matt's face. He took the hint and kissed her long enough for the minister to clear his throat. The organist gave them a hint by playing the recessional.

"I love you, my Christmas Angel," Matt said.

The Christmas Promise

Mary Marvella

The darkness of terror seeped into Beth's soul. Her body was stone heavy and unmovable. Hands like steel bands squeezed her throat, choking. *No air!*

"I can kill you and no one will know. No one can stop me." Her attacker's voice echoed in her head, made her struggle harder against the weight of his bulk.

One hand held her throat while a meaty fist slammed into her jaw. She tasted her own blood. The knee in her groin dug, crushing her bladder. *Just don't let him rape me.* Any second now she'd pass out.

I'm gonna die this time. He's won.

The darkness didn't want to turn her loose. It finally did and she awoke, trembling and pulling great gasps of air into her lungs. Sun streamed through her bedroom blinds, pushing away the darkness of her nightmare.

Her sheets were soaked with sweat when she awoke. Her night clothes clung to her body, but she could breathe normally.

Or maybe she'd died and gone to a heaven where she could smell bacon and eggs. In this heaven her son singing Christmas carols reminded her Christmas was only weeks away.

"Mom!" David's baritone voice called. "Up and at' em! Rise and shine."

David was home. Her baby boy was in her kitchen cooking and singing. Had he seen his sister yet? Did he know about what his father had done only days ago? She almost hoped her daughter had done her painful work for her. How could a mother tell her son that his father, a man he loved and admired, had attacked her after a year's separation?

"Ma! Breakfast is gonna get cold. Drag it out and hug your favorite son. I got a surprise for you and Dad."

His Dad! "Coming," Beth called back. Her empty stomach dropped, but her voice sounded stronger than she'd expected after the nightmare strangling. "Coming, son!" she repeated.

It was only a nightmare. A nightmare she'd had every night for the past week. A nightmare worse than those she'd experienced during her twenty-five years in marriage hell. She'd thought herself rid of it and her controlling, violent spouse.

She untangled herself from knotted bedclothes and rose painfully from her bed, the one she'd bought after trashing the one her husband had used to try to regain control of her body and her soul. Never again could she sleep in the bed where she had endured rape and a beating. Chilled and still sweat damp, she grabbed her terry cloth robe, running a hand over the fabric smooth from frequent washings.

She had work to do, so she moved into the bathroom to put herself together.

Washing her face with cold water woke her but failed to do much for the bruising around her throat or the still-discolored eye. Gingerly she touched the tender skin on her face. Not as sore as it was yesterday. Black and blue had given way to green and yellow. Makeup wouldn't hide it yet.

Brushing her teeth was still painful on the side where Bill's fist had connected with her jaw and loosened teeth. The split gum no longer bled, but she still avoided chewy foods.

This week mirrors weren't her friends.

Many of her friends avoided her. She understood. What could they say? For years she'd hidden the truth about her life with the father of her children. David, her youngest, still didn't know the extent of his mother's suffering.

Tying her robe with trembling hands, Beth prepared to

tell her son what a son of a bitch his father had been. In minutes he would know she had put the man in jail. Her stomach roiled.

She padded from her room to the stairs, moving slowly in deference to her sore muscles. Each step took her closer to a task she wished she could avoid. Pausing on the bottom step, she heard David's strong voice, angry and confused.

"Why would you tell such a lie?"

She heard his fist slam the table and flinched. "It's not like you, Sue. How could you lie about the man who loves us so much? How?"

"Because the bastard beat the shit out of our mother!"

Sue's vehemence startled Beth. She still waited, listening. "That's why. Daddy, dearest nearly killed her this time. He's..." Strong, oldest daughter Susan sobbed. Sarah didn't cry when she skinned knees. She didn't cry when she didn't get into her first choice of colleges. Knowing her mama was hurting and that her daddy was responsible made her sob for all she was worth.

"You're not making this up?" David's voice sounded young, vulnerable. "Sue? I gotta see Mom now. Is she okay? How could you not tell me before now? How could you leave me thinking everything was okay?"

Beth left the step where she'd taken root and moved toward the kitchen and her children. She'd waited long enough to tell her David the truth. Her son wasn't singing anymore.

Taking a deep, steadying breath, she exhaled slowly, then she pushed the swinging door to her kitchen.

Anger and pain, confusion and fear hung in the air, almost palpable, nearly overshadowing the food smells.

Susan's red eyes made Beth want to go hug her.

"David." Beth's voice was low. David's face was ashen.

"Oh, shit! Mom! Mom!" He moved to embrace her, then he backed off, as if he were afraid he'd hurt her.

When she stepped into his muscular arms she stifled a tremble caused by the fear of a strong man. His tears wet her hair. His twenty-year old body had filled out, even during the three months he'd been away at school.

This big man was her gentle son, not his father. He'd always looked like Bill. For a second she'd felt fear in his arms, then she'd let it go. No way would she let Bill ruin her love for her son. So many times she'd held him in her arms. She must act like his mother, not a victim. But she was a victim.

Beth felt Susan's arms embracing both mother and

brother. "It's okay, Mama, David and I are here to protect you. We won't let anyone hurt you ever again."

"I thought that was my line." Beth pulled away enough to stretch up and kiss her son's beard-roughened jaw. "We need to talk about things. But first, why don't we try to do justice to this wonderful breakfast my kids prepared?" Her forced cheer sounded fake in her own ears.

"Susan, how long have you been here?" Beth tried to chew the perfectly browned bacon. Her gums hurt and the salt burned her lip cut. She could eat the omelet and the grits.

"Mom? You expect me to sit calmly and eat?" David stood beside his mother's chair.

Beth looked at him and tried to smile, like everything was normal, like she hadn't just told her son something unbelievable.

"But you cooked for us," she answered calmly, patting his arm. "We can't waste your efforts, and we need nourishment."

She turned to Susan. "Did you help your brother with this omelet? It tastes like yours." It also hurt all the way down her throat like she swallowed glass. So much for soft food being easier to eat than the bacon.

David perched on the edge of his chair. "Sue was

here when I got here. I drove all night. She said you needed us, but she didn't explain why." David wadded a napkin and looked at his mother then his sister. "Why in the hell didn't someone tell me about what's been happening? Don't you think I needed to know my mother had been attacked?" He clinched his fists. "How? Why? Was Dad drinking or something?"

Beth watched him battle with the questions hanging the air.

"You had exams to finish," Susan answered for her mother. "You needed to ---"

David's voice was a roar of pain. "But I should have been here. I'd have been here in five or six hours."

"That's why we didn't call you. There was nothing you could have done."

"You don't know that. I could have—have—I don't know. I could have stopped him. I could have looked after Mama."

"You'd have fought with him. I wouldn't want that. I know you would have looked after me, but Susan was here." Beth trembled at the thought of those nightmares responsible for her fatigue. "I sent her home last night." She gave Susan a look she hoped would let her know she appreciated her but she should have minded her mama.

"She didn't go, Mom. I woke her when I came in. I just wish I could have been here to help. Why would Dad do such a horrible thing? Why?"

Beth wished she could answer his question.

Susan placed her hand on his tensed arm. "If you'd been here you'd have done something rash, like beating your own father."

He shrugged her hand away. "If I'd been here Dad wouldn't have hurt her. If only I'd been here!" David's chair toppled when he jerked out of it. "Why'd he do it? I don't understand."

Susan stood beside her mother. "It wasn't the first time." She still skirted his question. "He'd hit her before. Mom just hid it from us and from everyone else."

Beth had tried so hard to keep the ugliness from her children. How long had Susan known?

"Dad's sick," Susan said. "He's one sick bastard."

Beth darted a glance at her daughter. "Sick?" God help Bill if he'd harmed her daughter. Had he...

Susan hugged Beth. "No, Mom, it's not what you're thinking. I heard you two arguing sometimes, but I didn't realize he'd hit you. I wanted to believe you really fell last year. I wanted to believe what you told everyone."

"Susan said Dad's in jail. Will they let him out until the

trial?" David's fisted hand hit his other palm, a gesture Beth recognized. His anger was building.

Beth heard the hitting sound echoing in her mind. Her pulse quickened. At that moment she saw a different face. David's face blurred into Jim's. Anger twisted the youthful features. She couldn't breathe. Fear moved into her blood stream and attacked her heart. Her world went black.

"Mama? Mama?" She heard Susan's voice from far away. "David, help me get her to the living room. I can't hold her any longer."

"It's okay, Mom, we've got you." Strong arms carried her, but she couldn't open her eyes. Whose face would she see? She couldn't bear to fear her own son.

"Do we need to call a doctor, Sue? She doesn't look good." David knelt beside Beth's inert body on the sofa, his big hand holding hers. "She looks really bad."

The panic in her son's voice pulled at Beth, but she couldn't climb from the depths of her anguish. Her son's anger had been enough to panic her. How could she tell him how fragile she was? How could she let him know he had triggered her collapse? Her hours of therapy so far were only a beginning.

Both of her children would need counseling, too.

So far Christmas wasn't looking up this year. *Dammit,*

Bill, you won't ruin another holiday for us. He had ruined most with his controlling temper fits or pouting.

Beth caught a whiff of Susan's delicate perfume as a damp cloth bathed her face.

"Wake up, Mom. I have some nice cool water and your pill. It'll help keep you calm. Come on. I'll take David for my counseling session. I think he's gonna need it before he sees Dad."

"Have you seen the bastard?" David asked. "How did you resist killing him? I don't think I can."

"That's why I haven't seen him yet." Susan knelt beside her mother. "Mom, it's okay. David didn't really mean it."

Beth tried to slow her breathing. Panic set in at even the mention of violence. Would she ever be able to control her panic reactions?

Susan and David led Beth to her shower and promised to stay near, in case they were needed. By the time she had showered and tried to make herself presentable, her kids were ready to set out to the counseling center for the help they'd need to deal with their anger.

Would she ever be able to deal with her own?

***

By late afternoon Beth was exhausted, but the work

she'd done at the family clinic had helped. A young mother who came in for a session had shown the symptoms Beth recognized from her own experience. During the wait in the reception area they talked. First came the polite introduction, then the *why are you here?* conversation.

Only after sharing her own story had she persuaded the victim to admit the truth. Beth shared so much more with the girl than she had in all her therapy sessions before or since she decided to escape her situation.

Seeing the woman cower when anyone spoke loudly or moved quickly struck a note of pain and rage in Beth. She questioned the young woman about the yellowed bruise marks on her wrists and heard the kind of stories from her that she'd told concerned friends and family years ago. The young woman's children's reactions when a male counselor entered the room were a dead giveaway. Desperation had made Beth share.

After an hour of crying and worrying about taking the kids from home at Christmas, they arranged a place at a battered women's shelter for them to stay. Maybe this husband would agree to therapy and get his family back. Maybe the wife wouldn't go back home until he had changed. Maybe she'd have to put the worry from her mind for now.

Beth's new-found strength during therapy had

angered her husband, the man who needed to control her, to make her fear him, to break her. He'd never gone so far or lost control before. That night his usual mind games failed to get him the satisfaction he needed. Frightening her had not been enough.

Even when he'd pressed her windpipe, cutting off her breath, she'd refused to beg. She refused to cry. He slapped her. When she cried out he felt like a man. He slapped her again, then hit her with his fists. This time she'd called for help after he'd left. This time she'd called the police, prepared to press charges.

Only his promise to seek therapy had saved her children the public humiliation of having their father tried for assault once before. When he'd stopped his therapy sessions she'd filed for divorce. She refused to bow.

Both kids were away at school the first time he hit her. She'd avoided the pain of telling them the truth. Now she had to be as honest with them as she'd been with the young woman who'd needed her help. Her own therapy sessions would do so much more good now. She was angry. Rage had filled her and spilled out, leaving room for her to heal, to take control of her life.

***

Beth waited for Sue and David to come home. They must have had one helluva therapy session. They'd left when she did and still weren't back three hours after she'd come home. A short nap on the couch had remained dreamless, thank goodness.

She still had to tell her parents and Bill's before she sued for divorce and before the assault case came to court, if it did. Maybe Bill could plead guilty and avoid a trial. Reports from the doctor who visited the jail regularly suggested otherwise. Bill still took no blame for his actions. He still felt he had the right to control her and his children with force.

Deep in thought, she nearly missed the sound of car doors slamming. Her children's voices sounded so different from when they'd left.

"David, Mom's gonna love it."

"I hope so!" David's baritone sang out.

"What the..." Her strapping son pushed the door open and carted a spruce tree through the foyer.

Bill had never allowed a real Christmas tree in the house. They were too messy and he said he was allergic. This year her kids were doing something they'd never have dared with their father home.

David propped the large tree against the door. "We need to start over, Mom. We bought a real tree and all new decorations."

"Yeah," Susan added. She dropped one of the shopping bags skimming the floor with their weight. "We talked at the therapy session about the way dad controlled our lives. The others in the group therapy session said they lived in fear of angering their fathers, too. Some had been beaten by their dads.

We'd never admitted we all cow-towed to him to keep his approval and love. Why didn't we realize it? Why did you put up with it for so long?"

"Yeah, Mom, why?" David cocked his head, looking so much like his father had when she'd married him, before she'd learned to fear him.

Beth thought before she answered. "Why? I'd always thought a man was supposed to be the boss of his own home. When your Dad showed approval he was generous. He worked hard. He spent time with us. He was a perfect father, unlike my dad who spent his time on the golf course when he wasn't working."

Beth shrugged, watching Susan. "Your dad was so smart he could make me believe just about anything. Who would have believed the respected Doctor was so unbending, so controlling?" Even now she felt the hurt his anger and disapproval had caused.

Susan sat in a chair, her chin rested on her fists. "Grandma and Grandpa thought he was perfect. They wouldn't have believed their son was mean. Did you tell Granny and Pops?"

Beth leaned over her daughter and kissed the top of her head. "Baby, what would I say? My husband gets mad if the house isn't perfect?" She cleared her throat to swallow the lump forming there. "Mama always kept a perfect house. His mother kept a spotless house, so by the time he started to threaten me, I had begun to believe I was at fault."

Wrapping her arms around her middle she gathered her strength to finish. "I needed to be a perfect wife and mother. It was what I expected of myself. That worked well for Bill. If he'd hit you or me sooner, I'd have made a move. I had just fallen into the rut of putting up with him."

"Not any longer!" David kissed his mother's cheek. "Maybe Sue and I can visit Dad before Christmas. I don't want to hate him, but I do now. He never should've hit you."

"If he hadn't, I might still be letting him intimidate me." We needed a subject change to liven the mood. "Hey, kids, why don't we get started on your tree?"

Together they helped David put up the new tree stand. They all helped him stand the real tree in the foyer beside the stairs. "Did he ever really love us, even when we were small?"

"I don't know if he knows how to love people. He knows how to control," Beth answered.

"Are you really going to press charges?" David asked.

"Are you kidding?" Susan asked.

"I have to," Beth said. "Besides, it's the only way I can be free, and it's the only way others will be safe, including you two."

"I understand, Mom." David hugged Beth. "It's probably the only way I can keep myself from getting revenge for what he did to you."

"He did it to all of us. You have to get past the anger and deal with it. Holding on to anger isn't healthy for any of us. It's time to move on and rebuild. We've got Christmas and a New Year before you go back to school."

"Well, Mom, I was thinking. I could stay here for a while and transfer closer to home next year. I could work and save money to pay for my school next year. I could ... "

"You could go back to school and finish this term. There's money to pay for school for you. Sue is close by so I can call her if I feel lonely. I'll even come visit you at school, with or without your sister.

"Maybe I could get her a date with some poor geek at school."

Susan threw a pillow and hit David. David grabbed it and held it above his head. He paused, then looked at his mother. He and Susan looked so guilty Beth laughed.

"Mom, we're sorry." Susan covered her mouth.

"It's okay. You can still act like kids." She reached for the other pillow and threw it at Susan. Pillow fights weren't allowed in their other life, either.

"I promise to grow up and stand up for myself. Don't you think it's time?"

Christmas Best Bet, Humble Pie

Mary Marvella

Atlanta, Georgia present

Chapter One

"If we don't stop working and go for food soon, you'll need to call 911 to revive me." Jonathan Brockton Hamilton III was so tired he could barely tell up from down. "Hey, fellas," he called from his office.

He stood on legs stiff from sitting behind his desk for hours. He extended his arms above his head in a stretch much overdue. He shut down his laptop and ambled to his door, then to the conference room where Drake and Carter hunched over one of many stacks of paper.

"You talkin' to us, amigo?" Drake drawled, pushing gold-rimmed glasses up on his head. He tapped his Monte

Blanc pen in a muffled tattoo on a stack of papers. Only he would use a pen like that for every-day work. For signing contracts for clients, that was a different matter. Of the three partners, Drake could be counted on to be the most designer brand conscious

"Nah, I was talkin' to the walls. Aren't you fellas starved?" Brock was certain his words slurred from hunger.

"Carter went into his stash of crackers hours ago and we shared 'em. I've been thinkin' of spreading mustard on a table leg and gnawing to make my stomach hush growlin'."

Drake leaned back in his leather chair. His blue dress shirt with his tie knot barely loose looked as though he hadn't been working twelve hours straight. "That man never stops workin'."

Carter peered over crooked reading glasses and rubbed his forehead, leaving an ink-smear over one eye. He'd pulled them from a bag with Bargains Are Us on it.

Carter dropped his pen onto his legal pad filled with notes in his cramped printing. "If you two are gonna whine, we might as well quit and go get a bite. We can finish this tomorrow and be ready to put together a top notch brief."

When Carter stood he looked even more rumpled than he had this morning, which was hard to believe, since he usually looked like he slept in his clothes. Could Carter sleep at the office instead of in the apartment no one had seen yet? Maybe it didn't exist. He was always first in the office and last to leave.

No one worked harder than Carter. He has shown more genius than Drake and me put together. The decision to offer him a partnership with no investment the day the three of us graduated Mercer Law School pays off every day.

Drake stretched his arm to study his Rolex. He squinted at the beyond expensive timepiece. "It can't be ten thirty."

"Yeah, it is," Brock rolled his shoulders. "I'm all done in. I'm callin' it a night and headin' out for a bite to eat. Want to join me?"

"Count me in." Drake rose and grabbed his suit jacket.

"Me, too." Carter rounded the long conference table.

"Wanna take one car?" Brock offered.

The three men strode out into the warm November night. Brock thanked the fates he'd been born in Georgia, where winters were mild and people were still friendly. Anyone within fifty miles of Atlanta could get almost anything he needed to make life good.

"Nah," Drake answered as he punched his remote to open his Beemer door. "I might get lucky and need my own ride home."

Brock shook his head at his friend's confidence. He probably would manage to pick up a woman for the night.

Carter unlocked his older model Ford Taurus. "Drake's got a point about taking our own cars. The closest place likely to be open is the Waffle House three blocks from here. You could get lucky there." He snickered.

"The what?" Drake asked. "What's so funny?"

"He said Waffle House," Brock answered. "Let's go, I've never actually been inside one."

He smiled as he pulled his Audi from the paved parking area into the driveway. The view of the spotlights aimed at the old house made Brock proud of the investment he and his partners had made in it a year ago. A November full moon shone above the highest peak in the roofline.

The old house needed renovations, but it would double in value in a few years. There were enough empty rooms for Carter to use one and save money, but he'd refused to take charity.

Brock took up the tail-end of the caravan down the street lined with old houses converted to businesses. If he hadn't been so damned hungry, he'd have suggested they find a nice restaurant.

Within minutes he pulled into a space between Drake and Carter. He saw not one gold or red tree near the building to show autumn lingered in Atlanta.

Brock and Drake followed Carter into the square, one story building. The room sported booths and stools. The noise level assaulted his ears, and the onion, fried foods, and coffee odors attacked his sense of smell. Actually, the whole room with its orange benches and stool tops assaulted his senses. Women of varying ages bustled around, some carried food to the tables while others placed plates in front of people seated on tall stools at a high counter.

Amazing, un-damned believably amazing that such a place could exist and that he'd never been in one.

Drake looked as shocked as Brock felt. Carter, however, caught the attention of a woman wearing a god-awful ugly brown dress and a striped apron. She winked at Carter and led them a few feet to a booth. While Carter lost no time sliding across one orange plastic looking bench, Brock waited for Drake to slide across the other bench, but he sat on the edge, as if he needed to be able to escape quickly.

Brock shrugged and looked pointedly at Carter, who motioned for his partner to sit beside him. By the time Brock sat, Drake looked to be in shock. Neither arm touched the table, but Carter wasn't so cautious. He grabbed menus from a holder at the end of the table.

A woman who looked old enough to be long past retirement age leaned over the table and swiped a wet rag across it. Never had anyone wiped a table after he was seated at it, even at the Varsity. Though Brock was ready to jump out of the way of stray crumbs, not one hit him or his partners.

Drake just stared.

The waitress gave Drake the once-over, then placed a set of utensils on a napkin for each man. She rescued a thin pad from one pocket and a pencil from behind one ear. "Name's Sally, and I'll be your server tonight. What'll you boys have?"

"I haven't decided yet," Brock answered in his courtroom voice that went with his tailored business suit.

"Well, you just take your time, Honey," Sally looked at him and grinned, showing the gap of a missing incisor.

"We'd all like water, please," Carter said.

"With lemon?" the waitress asked.

At his nod she asked. "Coffee?"

"God, yes," Carter said. "I could use a gallon."

Brock echoed his response.

When she left to get their water Drake muttered, "Probably should've ordered bottled water."

Though Brock thought Carter flinched beside him, he didn't bring attention to it. Carter took a glance at the plastic sheet menu and put it back. "I know what I want."

Drake glanced over the menu he held by the edges. Maybe he'd like plastic gloves. "What?"

Carter grinned. "I'll have pecan waffles with peach syrup and coffee, lots of it."

"Oh, maybe I'll have the same," Drake said, still frowning.

The waitress leaned over the counter at the end of the table to place their glasses of water in front of Carter, who gave each man one.

Brock couldn't remember having a waitress lean over a counter instead of coming to the table. Then she put cups and saucers on the table. He couldn't remember having a booth butted against a counter behind which the cooks cooked and waitresses grabbed food and utensils, either.

At Drake's frown, she said. "I'll bring you gents fresh coffee in a second." True to her word she bustled to their table, poured steaming coffee, and pointed to the sweeteners. "Cream?" she asked. She reached into an apron pocket and placed creamer packets on the table.

"Thanks," Carter and Brock said together.

"Yes, thank you," Drake echoed with a bit of attitude.

Carter got things moving by ordering. "I'll have pecan waffles and a couple of eggs over light."

Brock ordered a cheese omelet and hash browns. He didn't get those often.

"Scattered and smothered?" she asked.

"I guess," he said.

Carter laughed at him.

By the time Sally went through all the other sides he could have with his omelet, Drake seemed to have his attitude under wraps and ordered the pecan waffles. Looking around at the customers, Brock noted that Drake looked the most out of place here. Though some men wore nice clothes, none wore ties and suit coats. Even the November chill hadn't brought out coats or sweaters yet.

Brock couldn't remember ever eating in such a hectic atmosphere or around so many different types of people. A young woman sporting a nose ring and a blue Mohawk dangled a combat-booted foot beside a man whose clothes looked frayed and as dirty as his longish white hair and scraggy beard.

When Sally brought a stack of plates to the booth beside Brock, the aroma actually reached out to make his stomach growl.

A yelp drew Brock's attention. A young woman rose to

leave. She wasn't a person who would have drawn his attention, but he couldn't miss the yelp of pain when the burly man in the booth across from her grabbed her wrist and tugged. Carter obviously saw the interchange because he pushed against Brock.

Brock was halfway out of their booth when the man slapped his companion.

The jerk had gone too far. Brock had been taught boys don't hit girls and real men don't hit women.

Expectant quiet replaced the noise of conversations and dishes hitting tables and counters. Brock took three steps forward.

"Take your hands off the lady, now," he ordered.

"Sez who?" Jerk Man turned on Brock, though he held fast to the woman's thin wrist. "No fancy boy tells me what to do." The snarl in his voice should've made any man with good sense back away.

Brock kept his face expressionless and his voice even, though the burly man looked tough enough to toss him aside. "Just take your hand off the lady and let her go."

"Lady? You gotta be kiddin', pretty boy. Get outta my business." The or else might as well have been spoken. The threat was loud and clear.

Carter stepped around Brock. "Do like my friend said

and let go of the woman. You can't assault a person." He turned to the woman. "Do you wish to press charges against this man?"

Carter could really put on the lawyer official attitude when he needed to.

"No, I just want to get as far away from here as I can." Her voice sounded thin and full of fear.

"That bitch let me buy her dinner. She says she ain't puttin' out." With that he yanked on her arm again. More than one gasp caught Brock's attention. No one else said anything or made a move to help the woman.

A blur moved past Brock and Carter. Jerk Man fell back onto the bench, losing his hold on the woman. Before Brock could process that Drake had left his seat, he placed a well-aimed chop to the jerk's wrist and a fist to his gut.

"I hate hearin' a man call a woman a bitch." Drake dusted his hands and straightened his tie. "Ma'am, do you need a ride home?"

"Uh, no, thanks." She glanced from her companion to Drake and to Carter and Brock. She dug a cell phone from her large handbag.

"I'll call my brothers. One of 'em 'll come get me."

She looked to be in shock and afraid, even of them.

As if on cue, each lawyer extracted a business card

from his pocket. Carter gave his to the woman.

"Ma'am, you might want to wait inside until your ride gets here. My partners and I will watch out for you. We're lawyers, and we'll be glad to help you take legal action to keep that jerk away from you."

She nodded and scurried to the other end of the room where she could watch for her ride. Maybe she liked lawyers less than she liked the burly guy. Carter's softly spoken "ma'am" hadn't reassured her.

Carter slid back into the booth, while Drake headed toward the men's room down a narrow hall.

As Brock took his seat, Carter spoke up. "What the hell happened with our partner?"

Brock laughed. "Drake is into martial arts. It takes a lot to make him lose his temper, but when he does, look out."

"Never would've guessed that."

Drake returned, looking as though nothing had happened just minutes earlier. He did examine his knuckles but said nothing. He held his coat against his body as he slid onto the bench across from his partners.

This didn't feel like one of those times for a play-by-play rehash of Drake's rescue. A glance at Carter made Brock want to laugh. Gentle Carter's face shone with the glow of new hero worship. Drake narrowed his eyes, a clear indication he didn't want the admiration.

Their waitress hurried to their table. "Gentlemen, I'll get you hot food if yours is cold. Order anything you want, no charge."

"Food's fine, thanks to Drake the little confrontation didn't take long."

Brock enjoyed his cheese omelet, every moist bite. In spite of everything, not one scrap of food remained on his plate.

Carter ate like a starved man and Drake, of course, ate his waffles as though they were crepes.

The woman Drake saved rose when three large men entered. "You took long enough. I was scared. My blind date was awful, but three nice men came to my rescue. Can we go now?"

The largest looked like he'd make two of most men. "What about the asshole who hurt you, Sis?" he asked.

"He left in a hurry."

"You didn't call a cop?" another brother who could probably bench press the building asked.

"No, I figured my big brothers would handle things."

"And we will." The third guy led the way out.

Carter finished his coffee then waved his cup for a

refill.

"Those men will do more to the jerk than the police would."

"Let's go have a couple of drinks and relax for a while," Brock suggested.

Drake ginned. "Sounds like a plan."

Twenty minutes later they stood in the parking lot of the Hotlantis bar.

"Come on, Carter," Brock called. "Let's have a couple of drinks and relax."

"Yeah," Drake said. "You are not to return to the office and work. We could all use a break."

"Fine," Carter said, making Brock want to laugh at him. He took almost no time to play. He worked like a man driven to earn his keep.

The Buckhead bar was loud, even after eleven-thirty on a Wednesday night. Several men and women sat on tall red stools at the long, black bar.

All around the three men, couples sat at small round tables, staring into each other's eyes or cuddling. Brock was starting on his second drink when the noise level lowered enough for him to hear Drake whistle.

Drake's drawl became so exaggerated Georgia born

Brock turned to see why. "Would you look at that?"

"What?" Carter asked. He turned toward the door. He grinned.

Brock looked in the same direction. His mouth went dry. The woman standing in the doorway looked like any man's fantasy, with her long black hair and nearly nonexistent little green dress.

"Now that's my kind of woman," he said. "She's gonna look great on my arm at Mama's fundraising party next Friday evening."

"I really don't think so." Drake straightened his tie. "I'm more her type."

Carter snorted. "You two are so out of your league with that one. She's too good for both of you."

Brock couldn't suppress the feeling there had been a challenge or two issued there. No way would he let that pass. "Watch and learn." He stood taller and straightened his shoulders. He gave his partners a big confident grin. "Betcha I'll get her number and a date."

Carter shook his head and took a swallow of his drink. "Betcha don't. And if you don't, we get to set the price of the wager."

"And if I get her number or a date?"

Carter looked at Drake, who nodded. "You can name

your prize."

"Works for me." Brock ran his hand through his hair and smoothed his shirtfront before he started across the room.

The woman strutted toward the other end of the bar.

Her runway model hip action sent heat way south of his belt. He felt that slight sweat that comes with a testosterone increase, and he could swear he could feel her sexual vibes aimed at him. When he was close enough to smell her subtle perfume she turned toward him.

"Hi." He knew his voice sounded too low and too hoarse, but he couldn't help the natural reaction to so much gorgeous woman so near and so well displayed. Her green eyes matched her dress, but something about her expression seemed wrong. Well, duh, he hadn't even introduced himself.

He recovered and held out his hand, prepared to hold onto hers a little longer than necessary while he gazed into her eyes. Worked every time. "I'm Brock Hamilton. You just made my day." He cleared his throat. "I'd like to buy you a drink."

She ignored his hand. "No thanks," she said and turned back to the bar.

Now what? "You look like someone I should know."

That should work. It usually got him a smile, at least.

She looked back over her bare shoulder at him. Her green eyes held no warmth for him. "No reason you should know me. Now, if you'll excuse me, I'd like to relax and enjoy the drink I ordered."

Brock seldom needed to do more than smile at a woman to get her name and phone number. This lovely creature wouldn't shake his hand or even let him buy her a drink.

He reached into his pocket to withdraw a business card. Could she be playing hard to get, creating that extra mystery? He tapped her elbow and placed his embossed card beside her glass. "In case you ever need a lawyer."

She shook her head and picked up her drink. After a swallow she put the glass back down on his card. "I won't."

Finally he gave up and strolled back to his buddies. What would they want him to do since he'd lost the bet? How bad could it be, anyway?

Carter tried to look disinterested, but Brock knew better. He was just curious as Drake, who was grinning like an idiot.

Drake grabbed Brock's shoulder and squeezed. "Sorry, old buddy. Shot you down, did she? Maybe you aren't her type. She probably isn't impressed by guys with messy black hair." He straightened his jacket over broad shoulders then smoothed his tie, which was already perfect. "Let a man show you how it's done." Drake didn't bother to smooth his brown hair. There was never a hair out of place, anyway.

Carter's raised eyebrow meant he was thinking, which could be dangerous. "So, if you can't get her number, either, I get to name both penalties?"

"Hell, yes, 'cause I'll get it. And if I do, I win and I'll think of something good for you and Brock to do for me.

"Deal," Brock said with little enthusiasm.

"Deal," Carter said.

Brock tried to keep his observation of Drake from being obvious. He didn't want to look as though he thought Drake could win where he had failed. Drake strolled across the room and stood beside the target without looking at her. He ordered a drink, likely scotch and water, and pretended he had just noticed her. Drake was predictable, if nothing else, and he could make a full-on attack look spontaneous.

Carter sipped his drink and shook his head when Drake spoke to the lady in green. "No, say no," he muttered.

"Did you say something?" Carter asked.

"Nah, just talking to myself."

Drake faced the woman who still faced the bartender.

Brock couldn't hear what she said, but he could see her reflection and Drake's in the mirror behind the long bar. The woman looked annoyed. Drake looked puzzled, his brow definitely furrowed.

Carter's voice held a smile, which contradicted his serious expression. "He's striking out, isn't he?"

Brock didn't try to hide his smile. "Yeah, he is. In fact, he's on his way back."

Drake's walk back seemed to take forever, since he moved in slow motion. Brock tried to be a good sport about it. He couldn't. "So when are you going out with her?"

"Never. She's not so great looking up close. Maybe she prefers women."

Carter nodded. "Probably has BO and bad breath, too."

Brock couldn't resist rubbing it in. "Yeah and her voice is screechy and her teeth are crooked. Who wants a date with her?" *I do, I do!*

Carter drained his glass and left his barstool. "Looks like I won this one."

Brock narrowed his eyes at Carter. "Aren't you going to try to get her attention?"

"Nah," Ol' Carter blushed to the roots of his blonde hair. "if she didn't go for either of you, why would she go for me? I don't have the finesse you both have."

When Carter looked back at the prize both men lost, she looked back at their group and stared. Was she smiling at one of them? Surely not at the two men she had turned down. Carter nodded at her but didn't make a move to go to her. Well, Carter didn't seem to date or at least he hadn't mentioned having a date. He sent money home to his mama, so maybe he wouldn't try to date a woman who looked high-maintenance and worth the time and money she'd need.

Drake brought Brock's attention back to Carter. "What torture do you have in mind for us?" He grinned as though he didn't expect anything really awful.

Carter rubbed his chin. Not a good sign for either loser. "Hmmm. Neither of you two ever had a hard day's work in your lives. You've been sheltered from the kind of people you saw tonight at the Waffle House. I've worked places like that and worse. I don't think either of you could do it, but…"

Chapter Two

Brock gulped his Scotch and water and choked. He finally found his voice. "You want me to do what?" No way had Carter meant what Brock figured he meant. That would be ridiculous.

Carter looked deadly serious. "I challenge you to get and hold a job at a Waffle House for one month."

Brock turned to Drake, who laughed so hard tears streamed from his eyes. He'd never seen Drake let go like this. Carter wasn't laughing, a bad sign. Of course Carter was serious most of the time.

"Carter, you have got to be kiddin' me." He took a sip of the scotch. It went down more smoothly than the gulp had. "We have a business to run, partner. I can't possibly take time off for such a stupid idea."

Drake's laughter subsided long enough for him to put in his one and a half cents. "You can work nites." His laughter took over again.

"You're not helpin'! Don't encourage his insane idea."

Carter looked affronted. "Insane? So don't take the challenge. Of course you did lose a bet, but I wouldn't hold you to it." The way he said it meant Brock would lose his partner's respect if he begged off. Carter worked twenty-four-seven to make up for his lack of a stake in the original organization. He'd take a bet seriously, and he'd pay his debts, no matter what.

"Hey, I don't welsh on bets, but this isn't a real bet. Hell, the stakes weren't even set beforehand."

Carter shrugged. "True, you said we could set the stakes after the fact if you lost."

"He's right." Drake rubbed his hands together. "We get to set the stakes, and I think Carter's penalty is brilliant."

Carter actually grinned at Drake. "Your time will come, partner, once Brock proves he can do this."

Brock raised his eyebrows at Drake. "Oh, yeah, and I'll help him think up something shitty for you."

Carter gave him the evil eye. "Shitty? You have so much to learn about real life, and this will be a start."

The crowd in the bar had thinned. The gorgeous woman was nowhere in sight. Brock checked his watch. Midnight.

"I guess I'd better head home, since I'm due in the office for an appointment by eight in the morning."

"That's early, why not nine?" Drake asked.

Brock shrugged. "This client is too busy for our

118

regular hours." He paid his tab and strode toward the door. What had he gotten himself into?

Hours later Brock awoke in a sweat. Damned dream was vague. Carter had been in it and he'd made Brock suffer. That much Brock knew, but he couldn't remember the details. He remembered being in a Waffle House and lost. He'd wandered around in the building that seemed more like a maze than the small building he remembered from last night. He'd have blamed the nightmare on the late supper or greasy food, but that was hours ago.

***

The next morning Brock dragged to the office at seven forty-five. After his nightmare the night had gone downhill. He reached for his keys to unlock the door, only to find it unlocked. He should have expected that with Carter's car in the parking lot - no sleep, brain stolen.

When he opened the door no alarm sounded. Now that wasn't a good thing. He'd need to remind Carter to reset the door alarm when he came in early or at least lock the door behind himself.

The aroma of coffee spoke to Brock's headache. He'd downed two cups at his condo, but no one made coffee like Carter did. Some woman should marry the guy just for his coffee making skills. *Well, maybe not just for that, and what the hell am I thinking? Must be sleep deprivation.*

Brock made his way past the reception room and the offices to the old kitchen. Carter, bless him, held out a cup of coffee to him. Just like Carter to take care of his partners. Taking advantage of his good nature would be so easy!

"You look like hell. Did you have more to drink after we left the bar?" Carter grinned. He was obviously enjoying his partner's misery.

"Thanks," Brock took a sip and felt more human. "for the coffee. I couldn't sleep last night."

The client who had insisted on an eight o'clock appointment arrived at eight-thirty.

Brock heard him enter and greet Carter, who offered to show him into Brock's office. "No need, but I'll have a cup of coffee, black," the stranger ordered.

Carter didn't bother to correct the obvious belief he was a receptionist. "Certainly, Mr. Stein. Mr. Hamilton is expecting you." His voice showed no strain.

Mr. Stein didn't mention his tardiness or apologize but blew through Brock's door like a cyclone. He strode to Brock's desk before the lawyer could come from behind it. "Arthur Stein," he said as he reached over the desk to shake hands.

The man wore Hugo Boss and looked as though his personal hair stylist had spent hours on his white hair. He placed a fat folder on Brock's dark wood desk, then he backed up to sit in a leather captain's chair.

Carter entered silently and offered a mug of steaming coffee to Mr. Stein. Stein gave him a curt nod as he took it.

Brock moved from behind the desk. "Mr. Stein, I see you've met my partner, Carter Andrews."

At that moment Drake knocked on the doorframe and said, "Carter was fillin' in for our receptionist who isn't due in 'til nine, when we open for business." His voice held just the right amount of censure.

To Arthur Stein's credit, he showed no embarrassment at his faux pas. "Which of you will represent my business? Your mama," he said to Drake, "assured me you could handle anything I might need done."

Had the older man mentioned Drake's mother to put him in his place, make him feel like a kid who needed his parents to get business?

Brock smiled and picked up the folder Stein had dropped onto the desk. He leaned an Armani clad hip on the corner of the desk and crossed his ankles, putting his expensive shoes on display. In this case he could out-designer-brand anyone but Drake, who looked like a model for Hugo Boss.

"If we accept you as a client, you will be a client of the

partnership.

"You'll have the expertise we each offer," Drake said.

Stein raised a bushy white eyebrow and stared so hard Brock was certain he'd offended the wealthy, powerful man. Carter stood straighter and taller than he had a moment ago. One of these days he'd realize his worth.

The potential client reached out to shake hands with each lawyer. "Fine. Now I have business to conduct, so I can't sit around here all day. Time is money, and my time is very expensive."

Brock grinned. "As is ours, sir."

Arthur Stein left as he had entered - in a rush.

Brock watched Drake and Carter leave for their own offices. Neither had mentioned the stupid bet or Carter's challenge. *Why the Waffle House?*

All morning Brock worked at his computer, researching case law relating to patent infringement. His research convinced him that Mr. Stein had a valid case and he dictated an acceptance letter, detailing the litigation process and enclosing a draft complaint. The draft complaint was more work than he'd normally put in to win a case, but Stein's attitude needed some finite alteration, as anyone skilled in the art would likely know. The last phrase had stuck in his mind from the past few hours on *WestLaw*.

At odd moments he remembered the dream about being lost in the Waffle House that had left him exhausted.

The ringing phone took Brock from his work. He grabbed it to save his ears from the punishment of the ring.

With no preamble or greeting, the caller jumped in. "Well, did Arthur hire you?" a woman's stern voice asked, as though she feared he might not.

Why would Drake's mother call him? Had she sent the client, thinking Brock would see him?

Brock ran a hand through his hair. "Yes, Ma'am, we met with him," he answered, keeping his voice even.

"Oh," She paused. "Brock, I was calling my son." Her tone became more genteel. "I thought he would see Arthur."

"No, ma'am, Mr. Stein wanted an appointment before our office hours, so I agreed to see him early."

"I sent him to Drake because his wife and I are on several committees together."

"Mr. Stein left papers for us to read. Drake and Carter and I'll discuss the merits of takin' Stein on as a client."

"There's doubt?" Her perfectly modulated voice rose and cracked. "You can't turn men like Arthur away."

"Yes, ma'am, I can."

He could imagine her twisting her southern lady

strand of pearls in agitation. "A young law firm cannot afford to alienate a man with Arthur's power. He could ruin you."

Chapter Three

Brock looked up to see Carter move into his line of vision. Stretching, he stifled a moan when a pain shot through his neck. He hadn't had a crick in his neck in ages. *How long have I been working?*

Drake joined them. "I've ordered take-out for us so we can work through lunch."

Brock hadn't realized how hungry he was, because Sandy, premiere receptionist and secretary, kept his coffee cup refilled. He'd need food in his stomach before he drank any more.

"Tell me you didn't order rabbit food and tofu." Brock grimaced, more because of the acid buildup from the coffee than the idea of Drake's usual health food preference. He wasn't a fan of health food, as such.

Carter grinned. "I wouldn't let him. I wanted to order fish 'n chips or cheeseburgers and fries, but our partner couldn't handle the grease. Wuss!"

The doorbell rang, then a voice yelled. "Food delivery!"

Drake left the room to get the food. Brock figured he'd sign for it on the company account. That way there would be no arguing about who would pay or individual expense accounts.

"Let's set up in the conference room." Carter led the way.

Before Drake could meet the partners at the long table, a feminine voice greeted him.

"Drake, are you boys havin' lunch? I thought I'd make Brock take me out to La Maisonne."

"Come on in and share with us, Miss Patricia, ma'am. We have plenty."

Brock's mom led the way into the large room. She looked as perfectly coifed as usual.

Carter hurried to pull out a chair for her and looked as in awe as he always did. Her pink Chanel suit made her look ladylike and intimidating as hell, in the way mamas can when they wear classic clothes.

He bent low enough for her to hug him and kiss his cheek. The telltale pink stain on Drake's smooth-shaven cheek showed she'd already nailed him.

Carter stood back. "Ma'am, can I get you a plate and glass? We have wine in the kitchen, too, if you'd like some."

"No, hon, I was teasing Drake." Mama captured Carter's face with her small hands and kissed his cheek, sending a blush over his face. "Just pretend I'm not here. Eat your lunch."

Three plates and utensils waited on the table.

Carter grabbed a glass from the wet bar and a bottle of Evian. "At least have some water while we sit."

Patricia looked around the large room and shook her blonde head. "This is a fine room, but not for eatin'."

Brock caught the excitement in her voice. Uh oh. "You must allow me to send someone over to fix up your kitchen and a dining room. As long as you have this lovely old house, it should seem more homey." She paced around the room, her hands clasped and a rapt expression that said she'd found a project.

"Mama, this is a place of business." When her perfectly pencil shaped eyebrow arched even more, he amended. "but we'll get around to finishing up the remodeling in a bit."

"I wouldn't meddle, but I know how busy you darlin' men are. I could get someone to prepare meals and clean up for you. Sandy has enough to do just minding your office."

At that moment Sandy's laugh announced that she'd returned from lunch. The carpeted floor muffled her footsteps, but nothing could keep her perfume from announcing her approach. "Hey, Mom," she said and hugged Brock's mama."

Brock thanked his lucky stars Sandy and his mama got along so well. Sandy was a good sport to put up with the crap Drake's dragon of a mother dished out.

***

The next morning Brock pulled into the parking lot of his office building as tired as he was yesterday. Last night he'd dreamed again.

In the dream he'd found himself standing in an unemployment line behind people wearing ragged, dirty clothes. Looking down at his own clothes made him want to cry. His shirt bore stains and his slacks looked worn. He couldn't remember how he'd fallen to this state. He just knew hunger pains gnawed at him and he smelled of nervous sweat. Desperation made the hand holding his papers tremble. What if he couldn't get a job? What if the person in charge turned him down for unemployment compensation?

No one looked at him or spoke to anyone. Each one shuffled forward, inch by inch. When Brock's turn came to approach the person who could help him, he caught his breath. Carter, wearing a new-looking suit and tie, sat behind a desk piled high with papers.

Great, Carter would help him. "Hey, buddy." He extended his free hand, but Carter ignored the gesture or misread it. *No handshake? Is he blowing me off?*

Carter looked confused then asked, "May I see your
128

paperwork? You're the last person in line, and it's late."

The man acted like they didn't work together every day. Hell, they must not, since he stood in this line and Carter sat behind this desk instead of the one at the law office. Brock shrugged and handed him the papers.

Carter shuffled through them, shaking his head. "Where have you put in applications? I don't see your appointment records or any evidence you're trying to get a job. Where were you employed before and for how long?"

Brock shivered from the cold sweat drenching his body. The papers weren't filled out. Why hadn't he realized it while he stood in line?

"I'm a partner in a law office. I have a law degree from Mercer University and graduated Suma cum laude," he couldn't stop babbling.

Carter raised his eyebrow. "You don't look like a lawyer."

At the moment Brock didn't feel like a lawyer.

Carter took a paper from his desk. "I have one job available." He handed Brock a job application. "The Waffle House is looking, take this and fill it out and take it to the one two blocks from here. They aren't looking for a lawyer, but you might be able to take food orders and wait tables." Carter shook his head. "A lawyer?" he muttered. "Right."

"I am a lawyer!" Brock shouted. "I am a lawyer!" He woke up to his own shouting. That damned dream had ruined any chances he'd get a good night's sleep tonight, either.

He dragged himself from his car at ten minutes before nine. From the second he opened the door to his office building he caught a whiff of coffee, Carter's coffee. Even the latte he'd bought on the way in couldn't spoil his taste for real coffee. At least the latte part would offer something besides caffeine.

He caught another aroma. Bacon? Waffles or pancakes? No way. Maybe his dreams were messing with his mind. Tomorrow he'd have his housekeeper prepare breakfast for him so his stomach wouldn't make him think of food.

Brock hurried past Sandy's desk to his office. He could resist another cup of coffee. In front of his computer lay a sheet of paper. A job application? No way could anyone know about his crazy dream. He didn't need to ask who had left it or why. Carter hadn't said anything lately, but the man never forgot anything. There hadn't been a deadline stated the night Brock and Drake had been blown off by the same woman, but maybe the time had come to try to bargain his way out of the stupid bet.

Sandy buzzed his office. "Carter has breakfast ready

for everyone! Drake just walked in. He and I are heading to the conference room before the food gets cold."

Brock would not be taken in by such tactics. He'd work and stay clear of the conference room and temptation.

Carter called his name. "Hey, Brock, come get some breakfast."

Brock didn't answer. He booted his computer, instead. Someone in this office would begin work on time. His stomach growled. He ignored it.

Carter stuck his head into Brock's office. "Aren't you joinin' us for breakfast? I'm treatin'."

"Did you stop by a Waffle House?"

"Nah, I came in early and cooked."

Brock's stomach growled.

"Sounds like someone's hungry." Carter turned away and looked over his shoulder. "Better come before the vultures eat everythin'." He left laughing.

Maybe a cup of good coffee would hit the spot. His stomach growled again. "All right, maybe we can eat something without givin' in. Gotta have a talk about the stupid bet. No way can I really spend my evenings working at a Waffle House or anywhere else. Carter will just have to understand."

After the office closed that afternoon, Brock brought out three bottled beers and frosted mugs. "We've done a good job with the Benson case. Let's celebrate. Or does anyone want champagne instead?"

"Nah, you got the good stuff." Drake popped his cap and poured his beer into a glass.

Carter drank from the bottle.

Brock followed suit and took a long swallow. "We've been busy, haven't we?"

"Yes," Drake took a long drink from his glass. "business is good enough to turn away cases."

Brock nodded. "We'll have to put in long hours here."

"Yes, and someone wants out, huh?" Carter asked.

"Out?" Brock asked. "What do you mean?"

"Someone doesn't want to go work at the Waffle House for a few weeks. I understand."

"You do?" Relief flooded Brock.

"Sure, you don't think you could handle it. It would be hard work and would spoil your social life, if you had one."

Drake drained his glass. "He's right, you and I weren't cut out for menial labor."

Brock shot Drake a look. Carter might find the statement insulting. "Hey, speak for yourself. I can do anything. I was going to offer to do something better, like make a big donation to the charity of Carter's choice."

Carter's smirk didn't bode well for either partner. He looked too sure of himself. "I don't know about charities. I do know donating money would be too easy for either of you." Carter nabbed another beer from the bar refrigerator and popped the cap. "Take the easy way out, if that's what you want."

He took a long draw from his bottle, then sat down and thumbed through a stack of papers as though he had nothing else on his mind. "You guys still work here, or am I the only one who has other cases to handle? It's all about billable hours isn't it? Let's make some money."

***

Carter showed no sign he was laughing at Brock while he checked out his job application. "Can't make it look too good or they won't hire you." He reached for Brock's silk tie and untied it. "Don't go in dressed like a lawyer or a rich guy, either. You can't take your car or wear that watch."

Riding in Carter's Ford Focus hadn't been as bad as Brock had expected it to be. Even knowing Drake waited in his own car a block away didn't help.

Carter mussed Brock's carefully styled hair and pushed him forward. "Go apply for that job. For God's sake, don't act like yourself."

That sounded like an insult. Brock approached the freestanding building with trepidation. He'd have backed out if Carter hadn't waited in his car. At this point Brock was thankful for the part of the agreement that prohibited telling anyone about this deal.

Jonathan Brockton Hamilton III walked into a Waffle House and handed his job application to a woman who looked older than his grandmother and thinner than a parking meter. She had introduced herself as Maggie, the manager.

Her fire engine red hair would give his mama's colorist hives. He waited quietly while she read over it. She nodded and smiled.

"Looks okay, but I can't believe you've never had a job before."

"I took care of my mother until she was cured of her agoraphobia. Now she doesn't need me anymore."

Maggie narrowed her eyes at him as though to determine if he was serious. The ancient manager nodded, then she reached into the top drawer of the scarred desk in her closet-sized office. She pulled out sheets of paper and handed them to Brock. "Pass these tests and you're hired. You got twenty minutes. I'll be back."

The temptation to fail one of the tests lasted less than a second. Carter would never accept that as an excuse.

The tests took all of ten minutes, five minutes each.

He dawdled for an extra ten minutes for the boss to return to call time. The acrid smell of cigarette smoke she brought in with her nearly choked him. He waited while she pulled out papers, obviously answer sheets, and scored his tests.

She grinned at him, revealing stained teeth. "Book smart and pretty, too. Perfect scores. You really ought to get into a college or technical school and learn a trade." She stood and held out her right hand. "You're hired, Jonathan."

Brock opened his mouth to correct her.

"I'll call you Johnny, if that's okay."

Good thing he didn't tell her his real name. Brock took her hand and shook it. Crazy, but he felt proud and pleased with himself. Of course it would be best to keep his identities separate. *Unreal. Damned unreal.*

***

Brock pulled the old Pontiac in the barely lit parking lot of the Waffle House where he'd serve his sentence. He'd give the car to some needy person later. His day had started at nine AM and included lunch on the run and a bagel for supper.

Hesitating outside, he rubbed damp hands on stiff khaki slacks. Every stitch of clothing still looked and felt new.

How could this be more difficult than taking a case into court?

He straightened his shoulders and strode into the Waffle House. Good thing no one he knew would be likely to stop in this neighborhood to eat. It was far from his office or the offices of people he knew. It was also far from his condo or those of the folks who knew him and what he did for a living. He must not see anyone he knew. That would require too much explaining. He had to keep it a secret, according to the terms of the "agreement".

Chapter Four

Each time red-haired, drill sergeant Maggie growled an order Brock cringed. Spending hours resisting the urge to tell her he wasn't simple-minded had given Brock a big headache.

"Since it's your first night, Johnny, I'll show you the clean-up parts of your job."

Brock didn't respond until he realized she was talking to him. He'd have to remember he would be Johnny here. "Isn't there someone who does that? I figured I'd wait on tables and such."

"Really? No, you can't start there." Her hoarse laugh grated on his last nerve.

All night he washed dishes. He reached for another dish to scrape, jamming his finger. Damn, his manicure was a disgrace, and now he had dishpan hands. When he asked if there was a dishwasher in the place Maggie laughed. "You're it."

He'd never worked so hard in his life or felt so out of his element. "I'll do my time for losing the stupid bet," he muttered, "then I'll get even."

He turned at the approach of loud footsteps and a

familiar hacking cough.

"Wipe down the counter, young man," the bossy manager rasped, pausing before the words young man. "When you finish that you get to practice putting utensils, I mean silver on the tables."

"Yes, ma'am, Miz Maggie." Brock grimaced. Sir would probably suit her better. She smelled of stale cigarette smoke and hairspray.

She grinned her missing-tooth grin. "Oh, shucks, we're fresh out of cloth napkins, Johnny, and I can't fold these paper things into pretty swans."

He shook his head. She didn't miss a chance to tease him about the expensive clothes he'd worn to apply for this job only two days ago. She thought he'd bought them at a second hand store.

Watching the clock became his favorite pastime by 4 AM. Customers came and went all night long.

He glared down at his grease-spattered clothes, new and his first purchase from a discount store.

His cheap shoes looked ruined, though the label inside had said they could be cleaned with mild detergent. Maybe his mama's housekeeper would be able to take care of 'em. But how could he explain why he had the shoes, or how they were ruined, or why?

"Git movin', sonny boy," Maggie reminded him. He failed to dodge the towel pop on his polyester clad behind. He'd call her on sexual harassment, but she'd probably laugh at him. So many people yelled sexual harassment when none was intended that he wouldn't have bothered. He'd turned down several cases he considered more a case of tight-ass overreactions. Besides, Sergeant Maggie had no idea he was a lawyer. *As if she'd care.*

She'd be dangerous in a locker room full of naked jocks.

He'd soon memorized the menu and was working on the terms that made no sense. "Covered, smothered, etc. Why not just say with onions, sautéed, or otherwise, cheese, melted, tomatoes, diced or sliced. He could spout Latin terms and cite hundreds of obscure court decisions, but the list made his head swim.

He clocked out at 7 AM, so tired he could barely put one foot in front of the other. One night of punishment gone and how many to go? By the time his sentence ended, he'd have a suitable punishment planned for Drake, who hadn't come to his aid. Then he'd get even with Carter.

Brock trudged into his apartment and headed for the shower. For the ten minutes he stood under a hot massaging spray. Then he turned on the side spigots. After the night he put in, he'd need plenty of water therapy.

He shampooed and soaped up twice, hoping the smell of cooking onions would have faded. He couldn't tell. The scent hadn't cleared from his nasal passages.

By the time he drove into the parking lot of his office he'd found his second wind. He'd pulled plenty of all-nighters in college, and he could still do it when he needed to. He could go to work now that the shower revived him.

There were three cars in the lot. Everyone would be waiting for his entrance. He grabbed his cup of latte and his laptop case, then he strode through the door.

The aroma of Carter's coffee assailed his tired brain, but Brock had no intention of going near the coffee maker. Brock steeled himself for a comment, but of course Sandy wasn't in on the bet. She looked around, sniffing as though she smelled something odd.

"Three messages for you," she said. He took the yellow slips she held out to him. Funny, with computer emails and voicemails, Sandy still used the message pads.

"Thanks," he said and strode into his office.

He enjoyed his latte and worked at his laptop in peace and quiet until he dozed off at his desk. The strangest dream sent red-haired demons chasing him.

"He must have moved into a bad position. His neck ached. His alarm jangled like his phone. He struggled to turn so he could silence the damned thing and nearly fell out of his desk chair.

The phone jangled again, the office intercom. He cleared his throat in hopes he wouldn't sound half-asleep, then he punched the speaker button.

"Yes, Sandy?" He punched random computer keys so she'd think he was working.

"Carter and Drake are in the conference room waiting for you. We expect Mr. Chambers in ten minutes."

"Thank you. I'm on my way." He snagged his jacket and headed for the bathroom next to his office. He spent two minutes washing his face and freshening up so he wouldn't look as though he'd been sleeping. If neither partner had bothered to stop by and ask about his first night at the Waffle House, he didn't need for them to think he couldn't handle it.

Everyone was all business as they prepared for Mr. Chambers to arrive. By the time Sandy brought him to join the team they were ready to go over his case and how the evidence stacked up.

***

That evening Brock stalled going into the Waffle House. He wore the second of five sets of work clothes and the shoes he had cleaned up from last night. At least he had a reprieve from asking his mother's housekeeper or his own cleaning woman how he could get last night's clothes clean. She tended to his laundry, but she had no idea about the bet. Surely she'd have a few questions if she found polyester work clothes among his stuff. Maybe he'd ask help from Carter's mom. Nah, he'd have to ask Carter, who would surely laugh at the poor rich boy.

The four hours of sleep he'd planned hadn't worked. The first hour he'd tossed and turned. The next two he'd tossed and turned and run from a red-haired termagant. That had left one hour before his alarm was set to go off. The thing had jangled for fifteen minutes before he dragged himself from bed to shower and wake up. The shower and a big cup of black coffee had helped, but his stomach rebelled at the acid and lack of sleep.

He should hurry into the place and do his new thing. After all, Maggie had promised she'd let him pour coffee for the men. Such a "thrill", since he'd get to keep the tips. Surely no one he knew, or would care to know, would visit this classy eating establishment.

Brock trudged inside to spend another day plotting revenge on the partner who had cooked up this torture and the one who hadn't helped him escape.

***

He headed for the high counter, where three customers sat on orange, vinyl-covered stools. At 12:30, in the longest night of his life, the long counter was almost deserted, but that should change soon, according to his ageless mentor.

No one moved, no one except the babe who glanced up from the stack of papers spread over the table of the end booth. The woman's pale, flawless skin looked natural. Her green eyes looked alert and bottomless. And she kept licking shiny, pink, lips, plump lips. She seemed to be saying something to him and he hadn't heard a word.

"Huh?" Brock's usual eloquence fled. "Ma'am?"

"May I have a refill, please?" Her luscious mouth smiled, questioning.

"Oh, yeah." Now was the time for his killer grin, the one he turned on when he wanted to make an I'm-a-good-guy impression. He reached for the glass she held toward him. Maggie was on her smoke break. He could do this alone. Ah, he grabbed the handle of a hose and pressed.

"Ohhh! Good Lord have mercy!" The lovely woman jumped as the spray of water hit her face and hair, dripping onto the table. "Damn!" Grabbing dinky napkins, she tried to rescue the files nearest her.

"Damn!" he said again. He started around the counter to clean up the mess. "Sorry! Wrong water handle. I'll help."

"No," she shouted, "don't come any closer!

Chapter Five

"Let me get Maggie, she'll take care of you. I'm new, so ..."

"No, thanks. I was ready to leave, anyway."

He'd never seen anyone gather so many papers so quickly. She threw five dollars on the table and bolted, carrying the papers and a laptop case.

"Give this to Maggie."

Brock stood, too startled to move or respond. How could a man who argued and won cases in court be so speechless because of a beautiful woman? In his own world he was never clumsy.

He let out a sigh of relief when he saw his warden saunter back from the "employees only" area.

"Well, handsome, get the counters all clean?" The red-head stopped and surveyed the damage. Hands on her skinny, uniformed hips she shook her head. "What didja do to Angie, she never leaves this early. She didn't even say goodbye."

Brock opened his mouth to explain. He waved the five dollar bill the beauty had left. He pointed to the place she'd vacated on the run.

"Never mind, I don't want to know. Just clean up the mess." Maggie shook her head. "It's a good thing you're a looker, boy."

"No ticket." He handed the money Angie left.

Maggie rolled eyes and grinned. "I'll ring her up and give her the change tomorrow. Don't worry, you'll get the hang of things eventually. Get ready for a rush, this place'll fill with the shift workers from the janitorial service cleaning the high rise office building across the street and we'll too busy to hear ourselves think.

And they were until his quitting time.

Maggie and Brock walked out to the parking area used by employees. He figured he was walking Maggie out, but she acted like he needed protecting. Daylight wasn't far behind them.

"See you tomorrow night, handsome. You'll get it right, eventually." Maggie waved as she left in her battle-scarred blue 1985 LTD.

Brock leaned over his trunk and removed a grocery bag. He glanced around to make sure he saw no one he knew. Silly, he'd never shopped in this area, so he'd never used this cleaners. Actually, he didn't take his clothes to the cleaner for himself. There was no reason for him to be sweating, but he was. He straightened his shoulders and strode into the Two Crowns Dry Cleaners.

The young woman behind the counter smiled at him. "May I hep you?" She twirled a long blond curl around her finger and gave him a red-lipsticked, pouty look. He couldn't believe she licked her lips and ran long red nails across her bare chest in a blatant flirting move. No way could he take her up on her offer. She couldn't be a day over sixteen, and he had no taste for jail-bait.

"You got your cleaning in that?" she pointed a long nail at his bag.

"Uh, yeah." He stepped up to the counter and made sure he didn't do anything she'd interpret as making a move on her. He plunked the sack on the high counter. "Three shirts and three pair of pants. Will they be ready tomorrow?"

"Just a minute, I need your phone number?" The girl blinked her lashes at him.

"Merry!" a deep masculine voice yelled. "Stop playing and get to work, girl."

"Yes, Daddy," she muttered. "Phone number, please?"

He gave her Carter's number, hoping he didn't do business here. "Will they be ready tomorrow?"

She gave him an eye-roll then picked up each piece.

While she examined each she shook her head. Frowning, she looked at the clothes he wore. If she had worked here for long she'd probably know the difference between expensive clothes and work clothes from Walmart. Carter had insisted he should buy cheap, since he wouldn't need the pants and shirts for long.

"You seem confused," Brock finally commented.

"I just wondered why you don't have your wife wash these at home," she said.

Could she be fishing to learn if he was available? Not to her, he wasn't. "I don't have a wife anymore. She always took care of my laundry." He shrugged.

She grinned and tilted her head. "Starch?" she asked.

"Uh, I guess."

"They'll be ready tomorrow afternoon."

"Thanks." He headed back to the office. He'd learn more than how to work at a Waffle House. Things would be so much easier if he didn't have to keep the bet a secret.

***

Brock had a night off from the Waffle House. He couldn't believe how grateful he felt to be able to work late at the office. As tired as he was, he would catch up before he left tonight. Running a hand over the smooth wood of his executive desk, he marveled at the patina of the antique.

He dropped into his leather chair and thought about the ripped vinyl seats at the Waffle House. God, he loved this office, and he hated working at a Waffle House! He really hated trying to do two jobs.

How do people do it for years on end? Carter did it and graduated law school with honors. He flexed his shoulders. By God, I'll show Carter and myself I can do whatever I decide to do. One month, I can handle it for one month.

Drake had already gone for the day. His mother had chaired a charity event and she expected her son there, looking handsome and well-heeled.

Brock laughed. Sandy denied having a crush on any of her bosses, but she nearly went into a trance when Drake left the office wearing a tux and looking like a model. Women seemed to like seeing him with his brown hair perfect and wearing his tailored clothes. The woman in the bar was the first women Brook knew about who had turned down Drake.

Barracuda Mother likely had invited a woman with political connections for her son to meet. So far Mother hadn't found Drake a woman they both liked for him. She wasn't just a typical matchmaking mother. She seemed obsessed about marrying her son to the "right" woman.

Brock strode into the office the next morning. A good night's sleep had worked wonders. He hadn't stopped for a shot of "high test" caffeine or even a double shot of Espresso on the way in.

"Morning," he called to Sandy as he passed her desk.

She glanced up and grinned at him. "You look chipper this morning."

Brock chose not to respond to that comment. If he did, that would be like admitting something was different today.

He sat at his desk and turned his computer on. He'd barely logged online by the time Sandy brought him his usual first cup of coffee. She knew him well enough that she didn't ask how he liked it anymore.

"Thanks," he said when she put the cup beside his elbow.

An hour later he heard Sandy's businesslike voice. "Good morning, Mr. Drake."

"Good morning, Sandy." Drake's voice sounded tired.

Brock rose and stepped to the door to see if his partner looked as bad as he sounded. Drake looked ragged around the edges but just as neat as usual – clean-shaven and not a hair out of place.

"How was the party, last night?" Brock asked.

Drake gave a scowl. "Mother had three hand-picked

marriage candidates for me, all eager and wealthy."

"And you got lucky?" Brock asked.

"And the one I drove home insisted on showing me what she had to offer." Drake's voice was so bland Brock wanted to laugh.

"You got lucky, then."

"No, I got laid, but wasn't so lucky. The woman tried too hard for a reasonably attractive rich woman."

That didn't sound like a compliment. "Reasonably attractive rich woman? What was wrong with her?" Only Drake could say he got laid but sound as if he'd been unlucky.

"Too much makeup, too much hairspray, fake breasts, and no real personality, to speak of."

Carter joined them in the receptionist area of the outer office. He must have heard the weariness in Drake's voice. He held out a cup of steaming hot coffee.

"Fake breasts? You mean they weren't hers?" Carter asked.

Drake took the cup as if it connected to a lifeline. He closed his eyes as he took a sip. When he opened them he looked better. "They were hers, all right. The best her dad dy's money would buy. She made sure I knew they were the best and that her dad-dy had bought and paid for them."

Something about the way Drake said daddy made Brock feel sorry for both Drake and the woman.

"Why did you take her home, if she was so bad?" Sandy asked, her voice full of censure. "You didn't do her any favors." She turned from the men to stare at her computer monitor.

Drake frowned. "Mother is running low on Atlanta Debutantes and is importing them from out of state. She had one from Charleston and one woman so young I wasn't sure she had all her molars yet."

Brock couldn't stifle the bark of laughter that bubbled inside.

When everyone looked at him, he shrugged. "Who was the lovely lady you took home?" He didn't really care, but he had to cover his rude reaction.

"Ray Ann Sat-ta-fi-eld," Drake said. He took a long swallow of his coffee, as if to wash the memory away.

"You mean the former beauty queen? The daughter of a senator?" Carter's voice sounded awed.

"Yeah, that one."

"You're complaining why?" Sandy asked, suddenly paying attention again. "She's beautiful and brilliant. What is your problem? What kind of woman is good enough for you?"

All male eyes stared at Sandy, who never scolded her employers. Drake frowned for a minute then grinned. "One my dear mother can't persuade to present herself as a marriage candidate for me. A woman who would spit in my mother's eye and say she'd never marry for money or position."

"Oh." Sandy seemed mollified.

Then Drake muttered. "Easy can be highly over-rated." He strode into his own office next to Brock's and closed the door, leaving everyone in the outer office stunned.

"I guess he told us," Carter said, laughing so hard both Sandy and Brock joined him.

Brock returned to work. He left his door open as he often did. With Sandy at work he could ignore all calls until she buzzed for him to pick up his hand set for a call.

Drake's impatient voice startled him. He must be angry if his voice could be heard through his closed door.

"Yes, Mother, I spent the night with Miss Sat-ta-fi-eld."

Brock caught a gasp from Sandy and swallowed his own at the man's tone toward his mother and the way he stretched out the woman's name. "and we flew to Las Vegas and tied th' ma-tra-mo-ni-al knot."

Brock flinched at the sound of Drake disconnecting

the line. Damn! The silence was so deafening Brock tried to pretend he hadn't heard the announcement. He waited for someone else to confront Drake. Why hadn't he said anything to his partners?

Less than fifteen minutes later Brock heard tires screech, the door to the house slam so hard he felt the house shake.

"What the hell?" he muttered and listened for a voice calling for help. He rose in his chair and started toward the door. He didn't make it far before a voice stopped him.

"James-Mont-gom-ry-drake!" A woman's high-pitched voice managed to make the long name sound an accusation. Mother Drake must have entered the building.

Sandy's voice sounded strained but businesslike. "Shall I let Mr. Drake know you're here, ma'am?"

Brock would give the receptionist a bonus for that response. There was no response to Sandy, just a bellow. "How could you!"

Drake answered her in a tone so calm he sounded as though he'd been sleeping. Not damned likely. He had to have known he'd lit a fuse under his mother.

"What can I do for you, Mother?" Drake's desk chair creaked. How odd. The chairs in this office never creaked.

Brock could see Mother Drake beside Sandy's desk,

looking ready to stroke-out.

"How could you marry that woman without telling your father and me?"

Brock could still see her in the outer office.

She pointed her finger in Drake's direction but didn't move closer. Maybe she was afraid she'd strangle him if she got lose enough. "What was your hurry? She couldn't be pregnant yet, could she? Oh my God. What were you thinking, James Montgomery?"

"Mother, you are makin' a scene."

At that she turned so red she looked ready to explode. She was breathing awfully fast, too.

"Since you keep throwing women at me, I figured I'd marry the one old enough to vote and buy her own liquor. The other two were infants and Ray Ann isn't getting any younger."

"You know what I mean, you ungrateful man!" She burst into tears. "You've spoiled everything. Her mama and I would have planned parties and a lovely wedding, a true society event."

Drake finally stepped up to his mother and put a hand on her shoulder. "Relax, Mother, before I have to call 911. I was tea-sin' you."

Brock stared at Drake. *Who stole our sensible Drake*

and replaced him with this crazy man, one with a death wish.

Mother Drake pulled away from her son and stalked out, tossing a parting threat. "Wait until I tell your father!"

When the door slammed behind her. Drake turned to his gaping partners and their secretary/receptionist. He muttered, "411, Mother. Father can't send me to my room or take away the keys to my Jag, anymore." Aloud he said. "No sense of humor."

***

Thanksgiving Day dawned unseasonably warm. Brock grabbed a summer-weight jacket as he left for his family home. Mama had declared meal times as dress occasions, and Brock dared not argue. So he wore his charcoal slacks and a matching sweater over his pale blue shirt.

All the way from his condo he thought about the past week of working two jobs.

Carter had been downtown since before dawn, working to feed homeless people. Carter was like that. His family would have their turkey dinner Sunday afternoon and Carter had invited both partners. This year Brock would be working at the Waffle House later tonight after he left his family.

What would his mama say if she knew? She'd likely

laugh and ask what he did to deserve this horrible fate. His daddy would laugh with her, but baby brother would have apoplexy and his high maintenance wife would have fainted! Hell, he'd enjoy that part of telling them all after he'd met Carter's demands.

He smiled at the lights decorating houses and trees, ready to light the area as soon as dark came. Early birds had already set out sleds and reindeer in yards. The closer he came to his childhood home, the more elegant the decorations became.

Then he saw the gate to the Hamilton estate. Everything about the place, from the brick fence to the wrought-iron gate, spoke of old money and dignity. What would the gardener, the grounds keeper, the maintenance crew, and his mama's decorator do this year? There would be no reindeer or sleds or Santa's waving. He'd never seen mile high letters spelling out messages of peace and goodwill to the passersby in this neighborhood.

Before he'd moved out to his own condo, he'd thought nothing when he'd driven through the stately gates. The place wasn't unusual or impressive, it just was. He pressed the button under the sleek dash of his Audi and started through the heavy gates wide enough to admit three cars abreast.

He grinned at the memory of Carter's comments the

first time he'd been invited here. That was the first time he'd realized he'd been raised in a mansion.

When he pulled his car around the circular drive and parked in front of wide steps, he let out a long breath. The large house with its wide columns rocked almost as much as his midtown condo. No cars waited in front of the house, but that didn't mean no one was here.

A young man Brock recognized as the butler's son opened the car door then took the keys when Brock unfolded himself from the low seat. The young man would move the car to a heated garage where the others were parked. He had barely reached the top step when the door opened and Jeffries stepped out. The man's silver hair had begun to thin. He looked the picture of dignity in his gray suit. But his signature Christmas red bow tie and vest made Brock smile.

"Welcome home, Mr. Brock. Happy Thanksgiving."

Brock enveloped the slender man in a hug.

When he ended the hug, Jeffries stepped aside for Brock to enter the warm house.

"The family is waiting in the blue parlor having drinks."

"My brother and her ladyship?"

Jeffries nodded but kept his expression bland. "Your brother and his wife have been here thirty minutes." The butler followed him inside, circling him. "Your coat, Mr.

Brock?"

Thousands of points of light spread from the chandelier in the high ceiling. Those prisms bounced on glass decorations on a ceiling high cedar tree beside the staircase. Mama's decorator had started inside the house.

"I didn't wear a coat."

"So I see." The disapproval almost made Brock smile. Many days Jeffries had met Brock and Jacob at the door on the way out, handing each his newest warm coat. Little brother Jacob had been a suck-up for as long as Brock could remember, but the butler always saw through Jacob.

Brock grinned when his mother met him in front of the giant tree. Her signature scent "Chanel No 5" enveloped him even before she hugged him.

"Happy thanksgiving, son." She hugged him and kissed his cheek, really kissed him. Unconcerned about smearing her lipstick, Mama never shortchanged with her affection to protect her makeup.

"Love you, too, Mama."

She pulled back and placed her hand in the crook of his elbow.

"We need to rescue your daddy from the *Prissy Twins*.

For two hours he watched Jacob act like a stuffy old

man, though he was younger of the two boys by three years. Beauty queen blonde wife, Her Ladyship to Brock, floated from room to room as though surveying her future home.

Neither of Brock's parents had been so stiff, but Drake could be. Ah, maybe Drake and Jacob were really related. Which of the boys had been kidnapped by the gypsies at birth? Maybe Jacob had been born to Drake's mother, the *wicked witch of the North*.

After dinner, Brock left with enough sliced turkey for sandwiches for a week. The cook had packed the leftover oyster dressing. The leftovers would be great at the office. No way his housekeeper wouldn't be insulted if he brought food to his apartment. She prided herself on keeping him fed.

When Brock left, Her Ladyship and the young master were still kissing up to Mama and Daddy. Neither liked Her Ladyship, but both were too well-bred to let her or Jacob know. *The Prissy Twins*. Good name for his brother and sister-in-law.

Jeffries held a coat for Brock. "Did you forget I didn't have a coat?"

The man shook his head. "You left this one here, and the temperature is dropping.

Outside Brock's car waited for him, already warmed.

Brock hurried home and changed into work clothes. By the time he headed to the Waffle House he needed the coat against the chill in the air. At least no neighbors would see what he wore this time.

Brock pulled up to the crowded Waffle House parking lot.

The warmth inside felt good. Customers looked up from their meals. Many greeted him with a smile and a wave. Two regulars called out to him.

An older woman Brock knew as Tessie asked, "Hey, Johnny, did you have a good afternoon with your family?"

"Sure did, both parents and my brother and his wife." Brock hung his coat on a peg, then turned to Tessie.

"How 'bout you, ma'am?" he asked.

"I'm havin' my turkey with Maggie and my friends." She gazed around the room, and he watched the other people smile at her.

How should he respond to that? Hadn't she mentioned having children?

"My daughter and her family can't come from California, and my son's in med school in Boston."

He and the short-order cooks exchanged greeting grunts.

Maggie bustled in from the walk-in refrigerator. "So, you finally got here? Folks been askin' 'bout you." She grinned as though she was genuinely glad to see him. She handed him a box then put four others on a counter.

"What is it?" Brock sniffed, itching to lift the lid and see.

"Sweet potato pie!" voices behind him chorused.

"I don't think I've ever had sweet potato pie. We had pumpkin pie at my Mama's house." He didn't mention the oyster stuffing or vintage wine or Her Ladyship.

He grabbed a coffeepot, the one marked regular, from the coffee machine and moved from person to person, refilling cups.

Maggie started a new pot then started around with the decaf.

Brock tried to be subtle while he watched the door.

Maggie laughed as she took and orders and gave them to the cooks. Brock had the dubious honor of taking some of the orders to the tables.

As he started fresh coffee around midnight, a small family entered. They spoke to no one but trudged to the back booth. Maggie took three glasses of water and coffee for the man and woman and a glass of orange juice for the small girl.

Each took a few minutes in the restrooms then left quietly.

They returned again three hours later.

Brock hesitated before asking Maggie the question hovering in the back of his mind. "Those people," He inclined his head toward two adults and child entering quietly. They brought in cold air and an aura of despair. "they've been in twice tonight. Who are they?"

Maggie's expression was somber as she motioned Brock closer.

"Billy Joe, the man, was on his way to a new job in Florida when their old car broke down yesterday. They had no money to fix the thing, so last night they slept in the car."

"In their car?" Brock stared at her. How could that be possible? "But they can't sleep in a car tonight. The temperature has been falling steadily since this afternoon. It's too cold, nearly freezing outside. Can't they go to a shelter or something?"

"They won't. That's why we don't say anything when they come in to use our restrooms and stay inside to warm up. Billy Joe swept up and cleaned restrooms last night then again this afternoon to pay for their meals, just barely."

Brock couldn't find his voice, wouldn't know what to say if he could. This should not be happening in a city like

Atlanta. They could get traveler's aid or something. "We can help them repair their car so he can go on to the job," Brock offered. "I could lend them the money and let him send it back later."

"Nope. He said he missed the chance, the job's gone."

"Well, we could take up a collection." I could contribute enough to get the car repaired and send them somewhere warm to sleep. "Or even go to one of the churches for a warm place to sleep."

By the time Brock trudged from the Waffle House, the restaurant had pretty much almost emptied. Maggie left as he did. She looked tired, but she should since she'd worked almost two entire shifts. A few early morning diners had stopped by for breakfast. Some families were obviously traveling on the holiday weekend.

Brock headed to his condo to shower. He planned to sleep a while. He wanted to put in some office hours today before going to the Waffle House. He had three more weeks to go.

When he opened his door the silence was deafening. Odd, since he usually loved the peace and quiet. He dropped his coat on a chair then started undressing, leaving his clothes when he removed them. He'd clean up after himself later.

After his shower, he wrapped himself in a fluffy towel, warm from the heated towel rack in the bathroom. He slipped into his terry cloth robe, also warm. He padded on the soft carpet to his bed and slid under the covers, exhausted and still damp.

He fell into a troubled sleep, dreaming of being cold, and hungry, and lost.

***

Friday morning Brock awoke to his blaring alarm. Eight? Felt more like he'd just drifted off to sleep. Oh, he had! He punched his snooze button. Just this once he'd indulge in a few extra minutes of sleep. An insistent buzzing woke him again. This time he punched the snooze button, but the buzzing didn't stop.

He cleared his throat as he grabbed his phone. "Hey," he growled. Shivering, he snuggled under the covers. He didn't remember going to bed naked.

"Good morning to you, sunshine." His mom's voice startled him.

"Mama?" He squinted at his alarm clock. Eleven? He jolted awake. "Mama?" he repeated. He really hadn't meant to sleep so late. When he tossed the covers aside he realized he had forgotten to reset the heat when he'd returned home after work in the wee hours of the morning. How had he missed the chill in the air last night? Oh. He remembered falling into bed wearing his warm robe. He padded to his dresser and grabbed clean boxers and an undershirt. He managed to step into the shorts using his one free hand.

He should have hit the speaker button but she wouldn't hear him roaming far from his bed. He actually slid his hand with the phone into one shirtsleeve, hoping he wouldn't miss anything important.

"What can I do for you?" he asked, then finished putting the tee shirt on. That felt better. He hurried to his walk-in closet to select winter-weight slacks. Holding the phone between his shoulder and neck he stepped into the creased pants.

"I was hoping you'd help me with my Christmas shopping today," she said.

"Ah, I had planned to put in a few hours at the office."

"But no one works on the Friday after Thanksgiving," she said. "Well, sales people do, that's why I need your help."

"And you didn't want to call my brother or his lovely wife? Mama, Her highness would love to help you." He tried to sound serious.

"Are you kiddin'? That woman and my whipped son stayed around long past their welcome last night." Mama never complained about anyone but the boring twins.

"Sorry, I promised to do a favor for someone." He hated lying to her. "Okay, I'll help you. When should I pick you up?"

"I'll be by your condo in fifteen minutes."

Oh, shit. "Oh? Are you already out shopping?" He hurried to grab the work clothes he'd dropped on the floor last night, figuring no one would be here before he could clean up.

"Of course. Jeffries is driving me around so he can help with parking and packages. He's a dear that way."

With every minute she shortened the time he had to get ready.

"See you in a few?" He hoped she'd get the hint to hang up.

"We can have lunch, too. See you."

He rushed to get ready and look as though he hadn't just awakened. He wasn't known as a late sleeper, even as a teenager. She'd figure he must be ill if she knew she'd awakened him.

By the time his doorbell rang, he was fully awake and had gulped down a cup of coffee. Why didn't she use the key he'd given her? He opened his door for her to enter.

She stretched up to kiss his cheek. "You're ready to go? Jeffries insisted on staying with the car."

"Sure." He grabbed his sports coat and his overcoat. "Is he listening to the UGA vs Tech game on the radio?"

She laughed as they locked his door and strolled to the elevator. Well, she strode and he sauntered so she could keep up with him. "It isn't on, yet."

He held the door open so she could precede him.

"Had you planned to watch it today? I can shop later, like tomorrow, if you'd rather stay home today." The doors opened and she gave him her Mama-loves-you look.

"Nah, let's shop." He put his hand on her elbow and walked with her to the Bentley parked at the curb.

Ralph, good doorman that he was, tipped his hat to them, opened the doors to let them out, then rushed ahead of them to open a car door for Brock's mama. The man knew he'd get an envelope of cash for Christmas, and he made sure he earned a fat gift.

By four in the afternoon, Brock had followed his Mama into so many stores he'd lost count. They both had gifts for Sandy, her kid, Drake and Carter. The fun part was done, and now they headed for the most expensive jewelry store in Atlanta for gifts for the royal couple. Mama wanted to select things the pair could show off then exchange if they didn't like 'em.

Brock wanted to suggest they head for Walmart and really shock her Majesty and her consort. Would Mama know about Walmart? Had she shopped there but not taken her sons?

When Jeffries stopped in front of Brock's condo building at five thirty, the street decorations were lit like a fairyland and his building looked like a magic place.

Ralph opened the car door before Jeffries could get out of the Bentley. Mama stayed in her seat and leaned to kiss her son goodbye. "I'll be by tomorrow to decorate your apartment and the office, if you'd like. Your daddy and I have a party tonight."

"Sure, Mama but I think Sandy plans to do the office Monday."

"Oh, well, see you for Sunday dinner?"

"I don't think, so. I'll call you." He was sure he'd be working at the Waffle House Sunday. "Love you, Mama."

He exited the elegant car and watched Ralph close the door, then run a gloved hand over the shiny finish.

By the time Brock made it to the office, he didn't expect to get much work done, but he wanted to try. Drake's Ferrari sat near the door. Parking near it, Brock grabbed the leftovers from Thanksgiving dinner and went inside. Drake had cut on the heat, thank goodness. Wednesday they hadn't needed heat. A concern nagged, but he couldn't put it into words. He'd figure it out eventually.

The quiet of the rooms disquieted Brock. "Hey, partner, you sleeping?" He wandered to Drake's open office door.

Drake looked startled, but then he seemed to recover his usual sardonic expression. "Well, of course not. Just thinkin'."

"Dangerous."

Brock sat back in his large chair and raised an eyebrow.

"Thinking, that is." Brock smiled. "Thinking 'bout what?"

Drake shrugged but didn't answer. "So, how was your Thanksgiving?"

"Good, very good. Except for my brother and his wife it was fine. Then, of course, I did part of my penance at the Waffle House."

There it was again, that niggling concern.

"Too bad you didn't marry "her majesty". She and your mama would love each other.

"My mother can't abide competition and your sister-in-law'd be plottin' an assassination of the queen. Besides, she reminds me of a black widda."

Drake said more but Brock didn't hear the words. Then it hit him. The family in the Waffle House was out in the cold last night. He'd slept warm, even without turning up the heat in his nice condo. How warm could a family be in a car? But what could a wealthy lawyer do about their situation without blowing his cover?

"Seen Carter today?" he asked. Carter might know someone who could help stranded travelers.

"The man said he'd be at the legal aid office today, doin' his duty."

"Well, it wouldn't hurt us to help folks in need. We can afford to." Why hadn't he thought of that before? Was he really a selfish jerk?

"Ah, nobles-oblige?" Brock just frowned as Drake asked. "What's really bothering you?"

"It's all Carter's fault. Last night at the Waffle House I saw a man and his family come inside to keep warm."

"You know there are homeless people all over. We can't help all of them."

"I know, but this poor man was on his way to a job when his car died. He and his wife and child slept in their car last night."

"Offer to help."

"Maggie said he won't accept charity. He cleaned the restrooms and the floors of the Waffle House for money to feed his family yesterday. He wasn't looking for a handout."

Drake frowned. "This job is really havin' an effect on you."

Brock shook his head and shrugged. "Nah, I'm still a self-centered lawyer." He forced a grin he didn't feel. If the job was changing him, was it for the better? And if he was becoming a better man, had he been a bad person?

With that thought he started for his office. Then he remembered the bag he'd brought in. "I brought food from home. I'll put it in the refrigerator. You're welcome to have some."

"Your mama's home?" Drake asked.

"Yep."

This time Drake grinned. "I'll have some before I leave. My mother's cooks aren't as good as your mama's. I could eat at your mama's house every day."

As much as Brock tried to work on research for a brief he needed to file, he couldn't concentrate. He finally did a search online for travelers' aid and ways he might find help for the homeless family. Several churches offered meals and sleeping space, but they weren't close to the Waffle House.

Maggie had probably done the same research. She was a worldly, wise woman. Brock had noticed that during the time he'd worked with her. She had grown children and had served in the army for at least ten years, according to her stories. How would she feel about him when she learned he had lied to her when he applied for the job and was still lying?

He still had more than two weeks-worth of lying to do. He'd promised to work with Maggie Sunday for half a shift. One of the waitresses wanted to attend her son's Christmas pageant at church.

He decided to head home and gathered his laptop. The phone stopped him. Checking caller ID, he saw Carter's cell. "Hey, partner. How was your day?"

The long pause made Brock wonder. Had Carter hit a wrong number or what?

"Good, thanks for asking. I helped cook and cleaned up all day Thanksgiving Day and spent most of the day today at Legal aid. How was yours?"

"I did family time with my folks and spent some time here at the office. Drake worked, too."

"Cool, look, my mama's cooking Thanksgiving Dinner for all of us at my place. Want to come?"

"Sure, what time?"

"Probably around five. Let me ask her. Is Drake still there?"

"He just left."

"I'll call his cell."

Well, well, so he'd finally see Carter's apartment.

***

By the time Brock went to work at the Waffle House, he thanked his lucky stars for the car heater. Would the homeless family still be on their own?

When he walked inside he got his answer. Billy was sweeping the dining area of the Waffle House when Brock arrived for work shortly after ten that evening. A four-hour nap had recharged Brock's batteries.

The place looked different with "snow" dusted windows and fake poinsettias. In a back corner stood the tackiest Christmas tree he'd ever seen. Brock stopped to watch Billy's small daughter standing beside Maggie, smiling at the plastic monstrosity. Little Marie tapped Maggie who bent to the child's level. The girl cupped her hand beside her mouth to whisper in Maggie's ear.

Maggie laughed loudly. The child looked startled. "Course you can touch the decorations, Sugar." In that moment Brock almost forgot the fire-haired drill sergeant-tyrant from last week, almost.

"Well, boy, quit your gawkin' and get to work. You never seen a Christmas tree before?"

"Yes, Ma'am."

Billy Joe and his family disappeared again and within minutes Brock missed them. The kid was a cute little mite, shy like her nearly invisible mother, Sue. Sue was looking so peaked Maggie talked her into drinking an extra glass of orange juice. He hoped they weren't too cold. Everything they owned was in a car that wouldn't run.

There had to be something he could do to help these people. His mother would know where to get them clothes, a house, food, or whatever they needed, but she had no idea he was working here. Besides, she'd have overwhelmed the shy people. He should know how to help this family and others like them.

"Maggie," He leaned over to speak quietly to his favorite Hitler. "Why don't you hire Billy Joe and Sue as regular workers. They seem honest and willing. How will they get on with their lives with him just sweeping floors?"

She put a tray of saltshakers in front of him and he helped her use the large salt container to fill them.

"Well, you see, neither of 'em can read enough. We give Billy Joe the cleaning materials he needs and tell him what he needs to know about how to use each one. They can't exactly afford daycare for little Marie. Sue washed dishes yesterday, but I made her rest today. Can't have her handling things if she's sick."

"Maggie, do you usually hire people to clean?"

She laughed her from-the-gut laugh. "Son, when Billy Joe doesn't show up, you get to sweep and clean and wash all your own dishes again."

After they finished filling the saltshakers, she placed another tray with peppershakers and a large pepper can. The new rush of customers came in as Brock filled the last shaker. Everyone stayed too busy to talk about Billy Joe's family, but Brock couldn't keep them from his thoughts.

There must be something he could do without giving away his identity and breaking the terms of the bet. He'd be done with his sentence in less than three weeks. He couldn't wait for his day off from here. There were no days off from his growing law practice.

It was almost the end of Brock's shift when Billy Joe and his little family entered quietly and moved toward the restrooms. Poor Sue was dragging. Brock had removed his apron, ready to leave, when Marie walked to him and reached for his hand. One free hand clutched the rag doll she dragged each time he saw her. She tugged his hand but said nothing.

Squatting, he still had to lean forward to hear her whisper. Nodding, he picked her up and walked toward the garish tree. Marie reached out to touch the blinking star on top. Her warm, thin body trembled in excitement. He needed a free hand to wipe moisture gathering in his eyes but blinked instead. His throat constricted when she hugged him and kissed his stubble-roughened cheek.

"Thank you, Mister," she said clearly.

Reluctantly he allowed the sweet child to stand, but not 'til he'd hugged her back.

***

His partners had beaten him to the office. The nattily dressed Carter, who was already in the office, grinned. Brock tried to smile back as though he hadn't worked twenty hours straight.

Carter sniffed. "Like your new cologne, eau de Waffle House?"

"Very funny, Carter. I'm due in court in an hour. Where's our partner?"

"In his office, Drake was here ahead of me, as usual."

Carter and Brock turned toward their partner.

Drake looked up from the folder he was reading and smiled at Carter. "Looks like our partner had a long night. Circles under his eyes, skin's a little pasty, too."

"Shouldn't party so late, my man." Carter chuckled.

"Thanks." Brock didn't bother to disguise the sarcasm. He walked into his office and was out in five minutes, briefcase in hand, hair styled. He only smelled like he'd worked with fast food all night. No time for a shower, shampoo, and blow-dry styling.

Chapter Six

The next evening he found himself watching Billy Joe and his family. On the way in he'd hoped someone had fixed the man's problems. The only person Brock could remember needing help he couldn't give was Carter. From the first night he and Drake had seen Carter working late in a restaurant, he and Drake had offered to lend him tuition or whatever he needed. Carter had taught the rich boys about pride.

"Maggie, are you sure we can't get Billy Joe to let us help him and his family? I can afford a couple of nights in a motel. I know a fellow who could find him a job."

Maggie gave him her narrowed eye look. "You might know someone? Why aren't you workin' for that someone instead of here."

Good question. "The fellow's my cousin and we don't get along real well. Anyway, it's not my kind of job, but Billy Joe needs the money, doesn't he?"

"I already tried that. My son woulda hired him, at least for the holidays, but we couldn't figure what to do about his wife and little Marie. He can't leave them in the car, and it won't run to take him to a job, anyway. He refuses to be beholden to anyone.

"Can we at least send them to their car with bottled water and food they can eat cold. They're bound to get hungry more often than they come in here."

Maggie shook her red head at him. "I carried a couple of jugs of water and followed them to their car. Some of my regular customers pushed it to the parking lot a block away. I know the security guard. He said they could stay a couple of nights and their stuff would be safe. The owner wouldn't know, but someone who parks there regular-like might report 'em as vagrants. Tonight they'll move the car to our parking lot so they'll be closer."

"You do know they can't live this way for long."

"Yeah," she rubbed her chin. "we'll figure out something."

***

Lawyer by day, Waffle House employee by night. Leading a double life was wearing Brock down. He worried about little Marie and tried to figure how he could get Sue to a doctor. Maggie said Sue probably didn't have anything catching, just a bad case of anemia or pure exhaustion. She acted more like she had walking pneumonia. Brock remembered having it himself just from studying too much and resting too little. He'd at least had healthy food and a warm place to live.

He stepped under a deluge of hot, soothing water. As

he dried with warmed towels he felt guilty. How could a man live in such luxury and not be able to find a way to help a homeless family? It he hadn't taken the job at the Waffle House would he ever have realized there were good people in need?

He then crawled between the smooth sheets of his king-sized bed. He dreamed about the family. They stood outside windows looking in, like the little girl in a movie he remembered from childhood, *The Little Match Girl*. They curled up and lay in each other's arms, freezing in the snow.

"Stay awake" he yelled, annoyed at himself for not being able to get them to come inside and warm at his fireplace.

He tried to open his door and go out to drag them inside. An invisible wall stopped him. He banged against the barrier but couldn't break through.

Brock finally gave up on the idea of sleeping. He grabbed his iPad and made notes.

Living out of a car is wearing Billy Joe's wife down. Sue is looking sicker each day. There has to be a way to get past Billy Joe's pride. The first priority is to get help for Sue. He wrote that down. *The Second is to find a place to keep his family safe. The third is finding be a job for a man who couldn't read.* He wrote those down also.

Marie would have a tree of her own this Christmas

and gifts. Then Billy Joe and Sue needed to learn to read. His list of things to fix was growing but it felt good.

Then he went back to bed and slept.

The next morning he arrived at the office in time to see Carter's Taurus and Drake's jag turn the corner going from the office. How odd. Well, no one expected any of the partners to sign in or out.

He walked in, his mouth watering for the coffee he smelled. He knew one thing Carter had done before he left. Surely he didn't come in just to do that. Sandy sat at her desk, holding down the fort. "Mornin', boss."

That greeting from her always made him laugh because of her cheeky grin when she said it. She stood and handed Brock his pink message papers. "Mr. Andrews is meeting your mama at her club."

He frowned. He almost never heard anyone call Carter Mr. Andrews. He nodded.

"Mr. Drake is playing handball with a client."

"Handball?"

"Squash or something like that. If he beats the client, we'll get all his business."

"Okaaay, thank you, Sandy."

By the time Brock put his laptop case on his desk,

Super Receptionist placed a coffee mug on a front corner out of elbow range.

He worked at his computer preparing two contracts that could make his firm a fortune if the prospective client could sell his prospective client on the terms.

Then he spent hours surfing the web to learn about agencies who could help get a homeless family a safe place to stay.

Brock finally had a night off, but what was he planning? Not Christmas partying or shopping for family or friends. He planned a quiet night in his apartment enjoying a couple of glasses of white wine and a quiet gourmet supper prepared by his housekeeper. He might watch a little television. He'd surely rest and relax, maybe zone out in his leather recliner, then sack out in bed, since he hadn't slept well last night.

He left the office, planning to go home, but he just couldn't. Instead, he made a U-turn only blocks from the office then headed back to the old house. As usual, he admired the tasteful white sign identifying the place as Hamilton, Andrews, & Drake, Inc, Attorneys at Law.

He soon strode down the wide hall into Carter's office. "Come with me, ole buddy. I need you to help me do something to help the homeless family hanging around the Waffle House."

When Carter just stared up at him, Brock ran an impatient hand through his hair. "I told you and Drake about 'em. Maybe you can help me get through to Billy Joe. You sure know about pride."

Brock was going to spend his free night at the Waffle House. How crazy was that?

Carter seemed thoughtful before he answered. "I'll go if our pal Drake will go, too. Get him."

Brook turned and headed toward Drake's office. "Drake, get your coat," he yelled. "Supper's on me." To Carter he said. "But we can't go looking like lawyers."

Carter laughed. "Wait here." He headed outside.

"He'd better not be running out on us," Brock said. "We definitely need him."

Carter returned, carrying a Walmart bag. Before Brock or Drake could ask what he had in mind, Carter pulled out three pairs of new, blue denims. "Best fit you'll find."

He handed a pair to Drake. "Early Christmas present."

Drake examined the jeans, nodding. "Right size." He took them to his office with no argument.

Carter tossed a pair of jeans to Brock, who didn't even waste time checking on the size. Carter knew his sizes from shopping for work clothes.

"Oh, fellas," Brock paused before he started his truck. "the folks at the Waffle House call me John or Johnny." Within an hour the three lawyers sat in a booth at the Waffle House where John/Brock worked.

All wore jeans and sweatshirts, also from Carter, instead of their usual Lawyers-R-Us suits and ties. When Brock introduced his partners to the other employees, he neglected to mention their law partnership.

Maggie reigned over the place, as usual, sporting her pins for her achievements during her years at the Waffle House. She grinned as she approached her employee's booth.

"Night out on the town?" she asked. "I'm glad you brought your buddies along, Johnny. What'll you boys have?" She handed each a menu, though Brock didn't need one.

Brock introduced Carter and Drake to Maggie, best boss ever. "These guys went to school with me." That was true.

"Great Christmas decorations," Carter said, grinning at Drake.

"I'll get you boys coffee to start off." She punched Brock's shoulder and winked. She bustled off.

Under his breath, Drake made a comment about the

plastic Christmas tree Brock had finally begun to like.

Carter gave his partner an affronted look then said, "My mother had a tree like that, except ours had homemade decorations and every single one we'd made in school or Sunday School. It was some tree." He grinned. "I might just unpack it and put it up at work, since I bought her a new pink tinsel one."

"You wouldn't?" Drake asked. He looked so shocked Brock laughed then looked at Carter, who wasn't cracking even a small smile.

"I would." Carter held his hand up, palm toward Drake as if making a pledge or swearing to tell the truth in a courtroom.

"You should," Brock said. "I think it's a good idea."

Both men stared at him as though he had grown a second head. He had shocked himself with that comment. The partners had already turned down offers of decorators hired by Brock's mother or Drake's.

They gave Sandy that privilege, and she guarded it. Her four- year-old kid helped, too. Brock's mom was allowed to assist, as long as she didn't veto Sandy's choices. Drake's mom wouldn't have offered to help, anyway.

Maggie brought coffee refills. They were finishing their refills when Billy Joe's family entered the crowded diner quietly, as usual.

Billy was soon behind the counter washing dishes. Sue wrapped in her tattered coat, huddled in a corner. Brock wanted to go to her, but Carter must have sensed his intentions, because he grabbed his arm to stop him.

Brock sensed when Marie spotted him. She ran to be scooped up, as had become her habit.

"Hi, Mr. Johnny." The kid's cute little lisp made her sound so delicate.

Brock stood. "Hi, Punkin," he said as he tossed her above his head.

She giggled.

"How's ya mama?" he asked.

She stopped giggling. "She's sick, real sick. Can you make her all better?" Her little face scrunched up as she touched her small hands to his cheeks. "Daddy tried, but we got no medicine, and he got no money for a doctor."

He felt an overwhelming need to justify her trust in him. "Oh, Sugar, I'm gonna try." He looked to his friend who was most likely to understand her daddy's mindset.

Carter nodded. He rose from his seat, grabbed his jacket, and moved to the corner where Sue huddled, shivering. He draped his jacket around her, over her own coat, and knelt to talk to her. They looked like old friends

186

having a pleasant conversation.

Billy Joe left his post at the sink, wiping his hands on a towel as he joined them. He didn't look pleased to see a stranger talking to his wife.

Brock held his breath, sensing that Drake did the same. The child uttered not a word.

"You can do it, partner," Brock muttered.

"Yeah," Drake said. "Carter can get almost anyone to do almost anythin'."

Brock chanced a look around the room and spotted Maggie. She didn't even try to seem disinterested. She placed her fists on her skinny hips and watched the interaction, curiosity evident in her expression.

At first Billy Joe seemed angry. He straightened his thin shoulders, fisted his hands at his sides, and took several steps away from the booth where his wife huddled. He turned and looked at her. Whatever she said must have hit him hard.

He bowed his head as if in resignation then nodded. All the starch seemed to drain from his stance.

Billy Joe walked as though each step took all the strength he could muster. He finally made his way to the booth where Brock still held Marie. "Ya friend sezs he can get my Sue help. She's awful sick." The man's voice cracked. "He said he knows someone who needs carpenter work done. I can't read much, but I'm good with my hands, and I'll put in a hard day's work for my pay."

Drake's eyebrows raised and his mouth looked slack. He looked to be in shock.

Brock grinned. "Yes, a friend of mine started remodeling his offices in an old house. He has extra rooms where a night watchman and his family could stay. There's a kitchen and ya family could have its own bathroom." Tomorrow would be soon enough to tell one person the truth about the attorney who worked at the Waffle House to learn about humility and caring.

"I don't take no charity," Billy Joe said in a voice so low Brock was certain he had to force the words out.

"Please, Daddy?" Marie begged. "Mama needs help."

Tears shone in Billy Joe's eyes as he nodded in acceptance. "Thanks fer your help." His voice was gravely, thick.

Carter came even with Billy Joe. His arm was around Sue. "We need to keep her warm." He turned to Drake. "Wanna get our car and bring it around?"

"Sure," Drake hurried out.

Billy moved toward Maggie and spoke to her. Whatever he said made her stare at Brock then grin.

She strode toward the small group.

Little Marie bounced in Brock's arms until Maggie reached for her. The child touched Maggie's face. "Mr. Johnny and his friends gonna help us. He got a friend."

"Yes, ma'am." Billy Joe looked apologetic. "Sorry to leave you with like this, but Johnny, here," He turned toward Brock. "and that Carter fella said his friend will let us work for a real place to stay. His friends'll help us with our car, too."

Maggie looked at Brock and Carter. "I knew our Johnny was a good one."

Billy Joe retrieved his coat and a duffel bag from a closet where he usually left them.

"Can we go get some things from our car?" Sue asked. "Everythin' we own is in that there car."

"Yes, ma'am, I know a fella with a tow truck. He'll bring the car to my friend's office. Called him already. We just need to meet him so he'll get the right car." Carter whipped out his cell phone and dialed. To Billy Joe he said, "Tell him where and we'll leave as soon as my pal gets back with our warmed car. Your wife and child don't need to be out in the cold."

***

Thirty minutes later Billy Joe's family entered the house that housed Brock's law offices. By the time the disabled car was sheltered in the garage, Sue was in the room which would serve as a bedroom. It now contained the pullout sofa from Brock's office and the family's belongings from the car. Drake had volunteered his coffee table, a gift from his mother. He hated it.

The doorbell chimed and Carter answered the door. Brock followed and shook hands with Dr. Ogilvie, Brock's family physician as the man introduced himself.

"Where's the emergency? You look healthy enough." He gave Brock a cursory once-over look then turned to Carter, who threw up his hands in a not-me gesture.

Brock took time to make introductions and led the physician to the room where he'd put Sue and Billy Joe.

Again, he made introductions. Dr. Ogilvee responded while keeping his council, though his bushy white eyebrows arched in question.

Marie stared up at the man while he removed his coat and opened his medical bag. She tugged on his arm while he donned gloves. When he stopped to look at her she asked. "You gonna make my mama better? Mr. Johnny said you would."

The kid had a grip on his heart. "I'll explain later," Brock said. "We really appreciate your coming out tonight, sir."

"For your family," was all he said.

He leaned down closer to Marie's level. "Yes, ma'am, I'm gonna do my best."

She took Brock's hand and followed him to the kitchen. She and Brock sat on stools, while Carter heated milk and made hot chocolate. Though Brock wanted to mention the million calories in the half-and-half Carter used, the kid could use some fattening-up.

Marie looked like she belonged in a commercial as she sipped her drink with a milk mustache.

"Where's Drake?" Brock asked when Marie held her arms for him to pick her up.

"No idea, but we're not saving him any hot chocolate." Carter laughed. "Someone drank it all."

Shortly Marie slept in Brock's arms while he sat in the office waiting room. She weighed barely more than a minute. She snuggled tight to him, as though she feared he'd leave her or someone might take her away. So much trust would have scared him shitless if her parents weren't only doors away. What did he know about the care and feeding of a kid?

He turned to Carter, who sat in the desk chair. "Making hot chocolate for Marie was a good move."

"Easiest way to put a kid to sleep." Carter smiled.

"Back at the Waffle House, what did you say to get past Billy Joe's pride?" Brock asked. He lowered his voice, in case Marie was a light sleeper. "Did you mention he could lose his daughter if DFACS got wind of their living conditions? I saw that when I was searching online."

"Nah, didn't need to. He loves his family more than his pride. He was almost ready to give up. I just asked him if he remembered the story behind Christmas. He said of course."

Marie took shallow breaths and whimpered. "Poor baby." He smoothed damp curls from her forehead. "Should she be sweating? Maybe she has a fever?" he asked Carter.

"Nah, she's just warming up." Carter shook his head, laughing at Brock. "If she had a fever she'd be hot and dry."

She whimpered again.

Brock kept his voice low and soft. "You're all right, Marie, you're all right." When she settled down and popped her thumb into her mouth, Brock thought his heart would beat out of his chest. *Is this the way a parent feels? Scary.*

When he looked back at Carter, Brock said, "Go on."

"I asked him if he remembered where the Son of God was born. He said, 'in a stable, of course.' He was giving me some hard looks, like he thought I figured he was stupid."

Brock nodded his understanding. He had watched Billy Joe work hard instead of taking handouts. He wasn't stupid, just not educated.

"I asked if his family was too good to let someone help them. If the Son of God was born in a barn where his family accepted charity, then could Billy Joe let his family freeze and be homeless when three men, wise or not, wanted to help his daughter and save his wife's health?"

Brock grinned. "And here they are. Good thinking. You're good, partner. Can't wait to see Sandy's reaction tomorrow when she comes in to work."

"We'll need to get our stories straight with Billy Joe and Sue and each other.

"Maybe early in the morning."

Brock's doctor came into the room, smiling, with Billy Joe almost dogging his heels.

As tired as Billy Joe must feel, relief shone on his face. "Doc says my Sue's gonna be fine with rest in a warm place and healthy food. He was scared she had the walking pneumonia."

Doc looked stern. "The B-12 shot will help her, but you need to make sure she takes the vitamins I gave you. When the sample packets run out I'll give you a prescription for more."

Billy nodded. "I'll make sure she takes 'em like you told me."

Had Doc figured out Billy couldn't read, or had Billy told him?

"If Sue doesn't perk right up in a couple of days, call me."

"We will," all three male voices answered.

The front door opened and a voice called out, "I'm back."

Drake hurried in, carrying large bags. "Someone want to help me with this stuff?"

Doc left as Carter went to Drake's car and brought in more bags.

"Santa carries Walmart bags?" Brock asked.

Chapter Seven

"What did you do?" Carter asked.

"Went shopping. If you and Brock can, I can." Drake laughed like a kid. "We needed a few things."

Marie leaned against Billy and watched the goings-on.

Drake emptied the bags on the large conference table. "Billy Joe, you needed sheets and stuff for your bed and the lady in the store suggested these things."

Billy looked as shocked as Brock felt. Drake had gone shopping by himself and at Walmart? *Dadgummed-mazing.*

Carter shook his head and took the bedding bags to the room with the foldout couch.

Drake couldn't believe how still Sue lay on the makeshift bed. At least she wasn't trembling beneath the tattered blankets, obviously brought in from the broken down car.

"A hot soaking bath would be just what the doctor ordered for Sue," Carter remarked. "Maybe some washing up for a little girl?" He handed Marie a bag.

Sue raised her head and sat. "I don't know how I can thank you and your friends, Johnny.

"You just did." A flush warmed his face. He couldn't believe a simple thank you would make him blush. Maybe it was Sue's sincerity that did it to him.

Billy helped his wife into the bathroom, with Marie tagging along, carrying the bag Carter had handed her.

Brock and Drake helped Carter make up the bed with the fresh new sheets. The helpful "lady" at Walmart had steered Drake well. Drake had bought blankets and pillows, too.

"Oh, wait." Drake rushed back outside then returned with a box. "You won't believe this." In five minutes the bundle he dumped onto the floor had swollen into a child sized bed/sleeping bag combination.

Marie slipped from the bathroom and rushed toward the perfect place for her to sleep.

"Don't you look like a Christmas angel," Brock commented.

Billy must have had trouble denying the child the long flannel nightgown Drake had bought.

Brock knew Billy'd have wanted to give the kid nice things. Hell, he wanted to give her nice things, and she wasn't even his child.

"Didn't know what size," Drake shrugged.

Marie ran to Drake. She clasped her hands under her

chin then reached for his hand. "Daddy said tell you thank you and he will pay you back every damned cent." She didn't seem to notice Drake's discomfort or shock. "Thank you."

She ran toward the small bed but skidded to a stop then turned to Carter. "Thank you," she said. To Brock she held her arms out and he picked her up. "Thank you, Mr. Johnny or Mr. Brock. I love you." She placed a loud, wet kiss on his cheek, then slid to the floor. This time she made it to her new bed.

Drake slipped from the room and Carter followed. "Night, Marie." Their voices were in sync. She snuggled into her bed and Brock eased into the hall.

"Drake, you old softie," Carter teased when they grabbed the empty Walmart bags.

Brock chose to pretend tonight had been normal for them all.

"Someone will need to get here before Sandy and make sure we get the story straight. In two more weeks we can tell everyone the truth," Brock said.

Carter laughed, and Brock figured it was because Carter was always the first man in the office.

"Night, Mr. Johnny," Drake said as he grabbed his coat and headed out to his car.

Brock rolled his eyes at that. "I'm gone, too." He

197

grabbed his coat and held the door for Carter, who was behind him.

Brock sat in his car for a minute before he put it in gear to leave. He couldn't ever remember feeling so good about anything he'd done.

***

That night Brock did not dream of Billy Joe's family freezing to death.

When his alarm buzzed he awoke more rested than he could remember feeling after only six hours of sleep.

Feeling lighter than he had in months, Brock hurried to the office. He didn't even take time for coffee before he left.

Only one vehicle sat in the parking area. Carter was already here, thirty minutes earlier than his usual early.

Brock entered his office and had to balance himself against a flying kid.

"Hey, Mr. Carter's fixin' breakfast for us." She backed up and twirled. "He's making pancakes, and my daddy's watching him." She began to bounce. "We took Mama orange juice and she drank it in bed, and Mr. Carter said you got two names, and we call you Mr. Brock when we're here, and we don't tell nobody you work at the Waffle House - and you look real dressed up." She finally paused and took a breath. Her eyebrows met over her tiny button nose.

"Well, munchkin, let's go eat."

She took his hand and pulled him toward the kitchen.

Before she could wind up again, the door opened and let Drake inside. He looked his usual perfectly groomed self. She reached her other hand to Drake who looked panicked for a second. Then he reached out to accept her gesture.

Somehow Brock would guess that was a first. Hell, she was his first kid pal, too.

Carter had set up two card tables and folding chairs for everyone. By the time everyone had eaten pancakes and bacon, everyone had instructions about keeping the big secret for the next two weeks.

When Sandy showed up to man the reception desk and keep the lawyers in line, Carter took her to the back of the house and introduced her to his cousin and his wife and child.

Sandy leaned against the doorframe to Brock's office until he looked her way.

"What?" he asked. The less he said this morning, the less he was likely to trip over a lie.

"Taking in Carter's family was awfully nice. Why aren't they staying with him?"

"Billy Joe will be doing some of our remodeling and can be like a night watchman. We have more room than Carter does, too."

Drake's drawl came from behind Sandy. "Are we workin' today or just visitin'?"

For hours Brock worked so hard researching two cases he didn't notice the time.

Sandy freshened his coffee, brought him bottled water, and his lunch. Several times he wondered what the little family was doing, but he needed to finish his project before time to head to the Waffle House and Maggie.

Occasionally he heard hammering. He'd check on it later. He might as well get used to having Billie Jo and his little family around for a while.

Yep, this would be his most unusual Christmas and maybe his best.

The End

For more books by Mary Marvella, check

https://www.amazon.com/Mary-Marvella/e/B008E1SJ32/

Mary Marvella has been a storyteller for as long as she can remember. She made up the "Let's Pretend" situations for the neighborhood kids. The arrival of the book mobile was as exciting as hearing the music of the ice cream truck, more, since she could check out books but seldom had the money for the ice cream. Her parents preferred letting her walk to the corner store for less money. She still pinches pennies.

When Mary's daughter was small, story time often meant Mama made up stories. Now retired from teaching the classic works of the masters, Mary writes her own stories and reads modern novels.

Georgia raised, she writes stories with a Southern flair.

Contact the author:

https://goodreads.com/author/show/4909455.Mary_Marvella

https://www.facebook.com/ARomanceCaper

http://www.MaryMarvella.com

https://www.facebook.com/mmbarfield

https://www.facebook.com/pages/Mary-Marvella-Author/121044561311561

https://pinkfuzzyslippersauthors.wordpress.com/

Follow Mary Marvella on Twitter @mmarvellab

https://www.amazon.com/Mary-Marvella/e/B008E1SJ32/r\

If you enjoyed this story, please leave a review on Amazon.com.

And on FACEBOOK.COM

Books by Mary Marvella

Haunting Refrain

The Gift

Margo's Choice

Protecting Melissa

Protective Instincts

Cost of Deception

Forever Love

Write Dirty to Me,

Her Deception

Cheerleader Dad

Weeding the Garden of your Manuscript: What Editors Wish You Knew

Haunting Refrain

Made in the USA
Lexington, KY
16 November 2019